HARI-jan

Ravinder Randhawa

Bijlee · **Mantra**

5 Alexandra Grove
London N12 8NU

Printed in Great Britain by BPCC Wheatons Ltd, Exeter

For

Pavanjit
Sukhraj
Harbinder (Nicky)
Kamalkeep and Panvandeep

With Thanks to
Aamina and Ali Ahmad
for their critique

CONTENTS

1

HARI-JAN

Endless begging, pleading, heart-rending appeals to her conscience – every tactic I'd ever heard of. And who was ready to break at the end of it? Not my frail, feminine mother that's for sure. Talk about the Iron Lady! My old Mum's made of reinforced steel. Though you'd never have guessed it to see her gliding round in her super-soft saris, *her hair falling down her back in a cascade of black curls.* OK, so that's Mills and Boon. Undiluted too. But she does have black hair and it is long and curly, and she won't have it wrapped up in a bun, the way a mother, my mother, to be precise, should. She just lets it all hang out and, kind of – you've got it!

I gave up hope, went silent, sullen. I am a hermit on a mountain top, I thought to myself, worldly things are of no concern to me. That's when she dragged me off and told me to choose. I did so with reluctance and disdain, you understand, these passing fads are so unimportant. It wasn't 'till I had them in my hands and saw Mum dishing out her credit card that an enormous grin came and planted itself on my face. Don't know where it came from, honest.

Reeboks! Yeah. Wicked and white. Huge and heavy. Took me a day-and-a-half to learn how to wear them. Now I could really get myself together for Pukey's wedding. She's my horrible smarmy cousin. I donned the super-glamorous outfit, arranged the shalwar cuffs so that they just tickled the tops, sequins and beads on silver silk, glinting against my space-age footgear. To complete the ensemble I experimented with my dupatta, draping it behind. Cloakwise, Mini-Batman running round her bedroom. Over a shoulder, very chic, except that it keeps slipping off and you spend all your time pushing it back into place. Tied around the waist, military fashion, ideal for - nothing much really. Lastly, twisted into a rope and wound around my neck. Aaaaaagh!

Problems? Confusions? Contradictions? I got them all and if you've got them, then FLAUNT them, is my motto! Not like my friend, Ghazala, who's taken to wearing a headscarf that practically covers her face, plus floor-length coats and twenty-four hour religion. There's a contradiction for you, calls herself the ugly duckling except she's the most beautiful girl you've ever seen anywhere – books, films, TV, art - the lot! You think the Mona Lisa's got something going for her, wait 'till you see my friend Ghazala; you think Michelle Pfeiffer's pretty well loaded in the looks department, wait 'till you check out my mate Ghazala; you think Princess Di's got a certain something, wait 'till you meet my pal, Ghazala.

We're friends because of the contradictions. Otherwise I couldn't be friends with her. I'd rather die a horrible death of slow torture at the hands of a sadistic tyrant who wants to rule the world. I mean, being friends with someone who is so yuckingly good looking isn't Plain Jane's idea of fun.

Guruji must have been late for chai-break when my turn came round. Mum said I was born in the middle of a baby boom. However I've decided to give nature a helping hand. I've been perming my hair, one strand a week, so Mum won't notice what's going on. You ever tried to do a surreptitious perm? Keep the gear out of Detective Mummy's way, the smells locked up in the bathroom? I have a slight advantage over most, I have my own bathroom. Yes, as you may have gathered, the family's got some dosh to slosh around. Not that you could ever suggest such a thing to me Mum, who raises her eyes to heaven when we beg for a 50p for the bus ticket, and starts thanking Guruji for his beneficence in the past, the present and the future. Like he'd left bags of gold lying round for us to pick up.

Supermarkets, that's what the family's into and I've worked them all. That's where I've had my real education – the evenings and weekends of watching a thousand different people and eavesdropping on a thousand different conversations. You hear everything and I mean everything, from the wino's to the church-goers, from the office workers to the UB40s, from the couples in heaven to the couples in hell. My old Mum know's I know, that's why she keeps her eagle eye pinned on me and on my seventeenth birthday she put me through the Indian fire hoops. Not literally you understand, she couldn't get hold of the right kind of hoops. And then what would the neighbours have thought!

My birthday had been that day and a very nice birthday it had been too. Dad was taking so long saying goodbye to his very favourite daughter and son-in-law that I retired to my bedroom where I could examine, evaluate and of course appreciate my pressies. Masi had given me a shawl she'd embroidered herself, it was really something! She'd designed it, so it looked really trendy. Gazzy's present, a cream blouse, was rather a puzzle, it seemed like it should be for someone over thirty with at least one foot in the grave. And she hadn't stayed long, nibbling a samosa and disappearing. We don't put nothing exotic in our samosas, I assure you!

There was a knock at the door. I looked at the clock. Midnight. No point in getting over-excited. With only two other people in the house, it had to be either the male or female of the parent species.

Mum it was. She'd changed out of her glittery hostess sari, and was now silkily draped in a dark blue and purple caftan, curly locks wafting round her face. God, she looks good, I couldn't help thinking, for her age I mean. I watched her, rather warily, as she sat herself sideways on my desk chair, elbows resting on the back, chin cupped in her hands, giving me one of her long, meditative looks.

"Sweet Seventeen!" she murmured.

"Thank you, Mummyji." She'd brought me up well.

"How would you say, life has treated you so far?" murmuring again.

But I sat up straight wondering what was coming. "Fine, Mummyji. Life's been alright." I'll let bygones be bygones. I'll forget about the fact that I never had a bike when all the other kids had one, that I have to toil at the supermarket till when everyone else was out having a wild time.

"There are times when we should look back and look ahead. Times when we should take stock, as it were," she paused. "It must be difficult living in England, yet being Indian."

I nodded wearily. How true.

"It must be hard to um ... *negotiate* between the two."

Mum's a businesswoman, she loves that word.

"But it's important, don't you think, not to follow the crowd, unthinkingly?"

Here it comes!

"When you're with your friends, Harjinder, what do you call yourself?"

"Hari-jan," and clapped my hand over my mouth.

"Acha!"

I'd gone and done it now. That steely sound in her voice told me so.

"If you knew more about India, more about the Untouchables, you wouldn't presume to be such a pagli. What I was actually trying to ask was how you see yourself socio-politically."

That's her BA (Hons) from Delhi University speaking.

"A *wog* and a *Paki*!" That's me speaking.

"Indeed. How narrow minded!"

Then she hauled me through a lecture on culture, tradition and history, the importance of being a whole and rounded person, and being able to be yourself. Very grand it was, except what it really boiled down to were even more rules and regulations. Like I didn't have enough already. This must be rule number 210 at least, Indian clothes only.

"I'll get laughed at in school!"

"Why?"

"Because ..." hating to admit it, "because they laugh at Indian things."

"Why do they?"

"Because ... you know all about it!" I exploded at her. "You know what it's like as soon as you step out of the door. It's like having to struggle through a fog of racism, sometimes it hits you bang in the face. Sometimes it's thin and vague, other times it's like everything's clear and shiny, and then up it comes

13

again, *bang, smack, wallop*."

"You'd better learn how to be strong."

Rule Number 211, Panjabi only. My response, "Don't need it, the whole world speaks English."

"And how do they speak it? Forked tongues Beti, forked tongues, those particular Indians knew what they were talking about. Your Angrezi does not say everything there is to say in the world. One day you may want to say to someone, 'I love you'."

"Mum!" I jumped out of my seat and hit the ceiling. Putting ideas into my head. What kind of a mother was she!

"That is not permission. Merely an example. I don't know what will happen to you. I have no control over your life..."

No control! And she's running the next best thing to an open prison! Drop me dead with a feather, as they say. I was so indignant all my words collided in my throat, and I was speechless.

"What I mean is, *Beti dear* ..."

That 'Beti dear' was said with so much sarcasm it could kill off a cockroach.

"...you may have occasion to express certain feelings and when you have this – occasion - you will want to do it with a certain style. English ..." thumbs down.

I'd better make sure I don't fall for someone who has a phobia of Panjabi, then what would I do?

"However, it's quite possible," looking me up and down, "that you may never have 'this occasion' I speak of."

"Mum!" I sounded like that stupid character, in some comedy programme who's always squealing 'Muuum.' I wonder about my Mum though, I really do, there's more to her than meets the eye. By this time I'm only half-listening as she rounds off with a lecture on the observance of all the social rules. Everything has to be *Ye Olde Worlde* Indian-style, else I'll be booted out sharp. Now, that's a thought.

My strategy, as usual, was to use my contradictions, and though I hated it I decided to stay on at school, except it wouldn't really be my choice if I had a choice. Some freedom of choice! Making me slog my guts out at 'A' levels. Mum wasn't pleased, but she couldn't very well say 'No!' to education and advancement. As far as I'm concerned it's my one way out. Out of the family way, that is.

Unlike my sisters, who left school early, worked the tills, then hit the marriage trail. I tried explaining all this to Ghazala, but she won't listen no more, and I think, though I hate to admit it, I was feeling a teeny weeny bit lonely. Perhaps that's why I got sucked up into the Beauty Contest. Not me as a person, you understand, but me as a thinking individual, with intelligence, a social conscience and the confidence to stand up for my views. Wow! Now that's what I should have spieled off to Mum, socio-politically speaking.

Happened like this. I thought I'd do something for the school magazine, *Spanner* is its name. So I wrote a poem, very funny and witty, I thought, about Mr Singh and Mr Patel at the seaside, frollicking in the waves. They're my people, I could poke fun at them if I wanted to. But the Lord God was filled with wrath and came down to see me, personal like, manifesting in the middle of the dining hall. Actually, his name is Suresh. And he's only half-Indian, the other half being of UK origin.

"This poem is extremely silly and what's more, it's

blatantly racist."

"It's not," I squeaked. I was in a state of shock you see. Him appearing just like that in front of me. He's someone who's a Somebody in the school. "I'm not a racist," I protested, rather weakly, and popped a forkful of shepherd's pie into my mouth to fortify myself.

"Some people swallow everything, hook, line and sinker," he went on, looking down at my well-filled plate. "I'm not going to print it. Here it is. You can put it under your pillow. I hope it gives you nightmares."

"Sounds like censorship."

"Think you're so bright and witty, don't you!"

Well yes, I did rather. I smiled smugly at him. "You're afraid to be daring." Sounded like 'darling'. I looked round quickly, hoping no-one else had imagined a mispronunciation. I got a shock. Not only were people eavesdropping, they were openly tuning in to our little - what shall I call it - encounter. An encounter of the literary kind. "If you suppress it," that's a great word to use, "I'll make copies and give them to everyone in school."

"And make a fool of yourself. Excellent!"

His parents were the highly educated kind. That's why he talked like that.

"Goodbye," and turning on his heel, marched out, without a single look back to see how I was seething with anger.

I was furious with him and with myself. I didn't get the last word. I didn't manage to give him the come-uppance he deserved. I'd lost to him and I was alone amidst a sea of laughs and giggles. Leaving my plate, so now I was hungry as well as angry, I went out to seek Ghazala. She'd be having her sarnies by the pond.

She listened, quietly, intently, not interrupting as most people would do. I wished she'd stop being so saintly and be my old friend instead.

"Perhaps he was right and it's not suitable for publication."

"Gazzy!" Yes, I know, sounds like you-all-know-who, but I'd been using it years before he shed a single tear.

"He marched into the dining hall. Told me off in front of everyone. Humiliated me."

"He probably didn't mean it."

"He did."

"That's silly. You're exaggerating. As usual."

"I'm not always exaggerating!" I protested thumping my hand on the grass. Eeek and yuck! Now it had mud all over it. "You expect me to turn the other cheek. What about an eye for an eye, a tooth for a tooth? He trampled all over me, in public." Why didn't she feel my outrage? "What about my IZZAT?" I wailed in exasperation.

Gazzy laughed out loud, shocking the ants carting away her sarnie crumbs.

That's my old Gazzy. That laugh put some heart in me.

"He could have been polite, Gaz. You gotta admit that. He could have done it quietly, privately. You know what it is," the socio-political light suddenly activating itself in my brain, "it's his big head. That's what it is." I nodded sagely. "It's gone to his head." All I got by way of reply was an apple. "The popularity. It's not everyone who's been requested to stay on as editor for a second year running by Popular Demand. And who was it making the popular demands? His girlfriend and Co. His

17

chamchas!" I could see the conspiracy clear as daylight.

Then I noticed something even more dreadful, coming straight towards us. It was VT Rice, decked out in one of her summer frocks, complete with necklaces, earrings, hair decorations and Shakuntala, her shadow.

"Hello Veronica, would you like an apple?" my Gazzy being all diplomatic.

"Thank you. I'm not Eve!"

"And Gazzy's not the snake!" Oooh I could've killed her.

"Sorry I missed the drama in the dining hall," settling herself down, arranging her skirts. Ditto for Shakuntala. "Are you terribly upset?"

"Goodness. Was there anything to be upset about?"

"That's good. No hard feelings then."

I'm gonna get him!

"Suresh is such a deep thinker, sometimes he forgets that other people don't ..."

"Don't think?" Cheap I know, but I couldn't resist it.

VT Rice sat up even straighter, fixing me with her huge eyes. "He thinks things through."

"He's passionate..." Shakuntala spoke.

Gaz and I looked at each other, rattled. Hearing Shakuntala speak was like hearing a stone suddenly start talking in tongues.

"... about our people, and about racism," she finished off smiling.

What's there to smile about?

"He has to be careful," back to VT.

These two working on a double act?

"He's the one that made *Spanner* successful. It's only because of his work that it won an award. He can't print just anything."

Not only did VT have starring role as 'The Girlfriend' she was also one of his 'star' reporters. She would be, wouldn't she.

"Bollocks."

VT looked offended. Ditto Shakuntala.

"He's scared, afraid, frightened. Timid," I added as a final flourish. "Wants to stick to the old-and-tried ways. Being a real goody-goody talking anti-racism twenty-four hours. Adds to your halo no end. But some of us want something more out of life. F.U.N. Fun! I bet he's one of those fuddy-duddies who thought *Patel Rap* was racist. But we didn't. Us *Jogesh* Public out there. We made it a hit." I was really letting go. He comes down to the dining hall and shreds me in front of half the school, then these two follow me out to rub salt into the wounds. Whoever said 'Love Thy Neighbour', didn't know nothing about this lot!

VT Rice sighed deeply. "I told him you wouldn't understand. You're the kind who thinks it's hilarious to kick your own backside. You're so loud and brash. You think it's clever to cook up trouble."

"There was nothing malicious in that poem," Gazzy put in. Her voice has gotten much quieter since she started doing her religious thing, but strangely, it'd got very solid, like she was really sure of herself. "And why shouldn't we laugh at ourselves?"

I was hopping mad, like a cat on a bed of coals. "If he's such a *deep thinker*," doing my best to imitate VT's voice, "I wonder what he sees in you."

"More than he'd ever see in you," getting up, genteelly brushing the grass blades off her dress.

And need I say it, ditto Shakuntala. They'd had

their fun and were going to walk off on me, just as he had.

"Oh yeah. Wanna bet on it?" Her superior manner just made me want to throw a tantrum.

They looked at each other, not even bothering to hide their grins.

"Give her a chance, VT," Shakuntala again.

What a chatterbox she'd turned out to be!

"What do you suggest?"

Cool isn't the word for VT. I felt like I was talking to a glacier.

"No no. You and your boyfriend are the *deep thinkers*."

"Um, let me see. A course in elocution and deportment?"

"There aren't any," my Gazzy trying to protect.

"I can arrange it. No problem," VT Rice smiled sweetly. "I'll be doing the teaching. And from your side of the bet, if I lose, I'll agree to wear those ridiculous *Rebbush* shoes."

She knew how to hit where it hurt.

"With a shalwar kameez?" I smirked.

"Very tempting. Almost makes me want to lose."

The bell pealed out for afternoon classes.

"'Bye."

They were laughing as they walked back into school.

"Gazzy..."

"Will you ever learn to think before you speak?" packing her bags and getting up.

"She forced me. No, she didn't," I had to be honest. "I wanted to do something to her, to him, to them."

"And who is it going to hurt in the long run? Who looks cheap and shabby?"

"It did happen quickly, and I wasn't thinking about

it really."

"Typical! You're always rushing into things, eyes closed, brain shut off."

"I didn't mean it."

"Then tell Veronica."

Gazzy it was, who started calling her VT Rice, after this ad on TV in which an overdressed woman with huge eyes, flounces around singing about VT Rice. And now it's V-e-r-o-n-i-c-a? Tell Veronica! I'd rather eat salmonella eggs.

VT Rice never liked me, not since nursery school when I learnt the alphabet first. VT's mother kept her indoors and tried to drum it into her, and got her so frightened she never did learn it. Her mother taught my Mum everything there was to know about English culture, how to hang the net curtains properly, how to set a table, though my Mother's never had *occasion* to set a table the English way, to say 'please' and 'thank you' every two seconds. And years later, when we moved, she came to see our new house with a smile you could see she'd fixed on with super glue.

Had I lost Gazzy completely? It'd been a week. She hadn't spoken to me. Whenever I approached her she just asked me whether I'd told Veronica or not. I haven't done anything, I'm not going to do anything. That'll be the end of it. I'm not playing VT's silly games. Gazzy thought the bet was immoral, it was disrespectful to another human being, it was a sin to tamper with a person's emotions. I could go on. Gazzy went on, when I managed to corner her somewhere. I'd be a graceful loser. But... I just couldn't bring myself to go and eat humble pie in front of VT and tell her it was a mistake, that I hadn't meant it. The mileage she'd get out of it would make me want to go into isolation for the rest of my life.

Retaliating for the sake of it. "What about when your parents force you into an arranged marriage?" I asked Gazzy spitefully, feeling hurt, wanting to hurt.

"They won't. "

"They could."

"I have my faith and I follow it. They respect that."

"Why don't you just go into an ashram? Escape from this wicked world."

"Muslims don't have ashrams or convents. You're born into this world and you've got to make the best of it."

"They got purdah," I purred. Ten points to me, I thought.

"You don't know anything about it. You only know what the English tell you. Am I in purdah?"

"You tell me! I don't see you anymore, you never visit, we never sit and watch films anymore. We don't go window-shopping, you don't talk to me, not like you used to. And you promised to take me to a Bhangra disco. You were going to organise it all, remember? Our alibi, our clothes, the transport. And that was last year."

"Things change, Hari. We can't be children forever."

"Excuse me grandma! I got to go chase me a boy before I hit me grave. Want to make a bet on it!"

She looked disgusted.

And wouldn't you know it! History repeats itself, almost. There I was having my lunch, feeling aggrieved, disgruntled and unhappy, forking gravy and mash into my mouth, when something came and sat opposite me. It's him, the Deep Thinker.

"Hello," he said.

I didn't reply. I decided to disconcert him by behaving as untypically as possible, openly looking up to stare long and hard at him and his clothes. What a hideous mish-mash of washed out colours, creases and crumples, one side of his jumper longer than the other, shirt collar falling apart so you could see the stuffing inside. I flicked a speck of dust off my sleeve, making the point. Question should've been, not what he saw in VT but what the hell does she see in him?

Let's get to the face. Actually, I can't get a fix on it. It's the wierdest face I've ever seen! It keeps moving, changing, shifting, going out at the sides, going up at the cheeks, going bent at the nose (not that mine's that straight). His face just couldn't stay still, one minute it actually looked ugly and the next minute there was something quite delicious about it. I felt like taking it in my hands, so I could hold it still and see what it really was like. My hand was half way across before I realised what it was up to. Oh shame, embarrassment, humiliation.

"Inventory over?"

"Uh, pardon? Actually I was just thinking what terrible weather we're having. All sunny and warm, forcing people out of their stuffy homes, and baring their all. Doesn't white skin look awful when it comes out for an airing!" I stopped and smiled innocently, waiting for the blast. "And smelly. Phooey," wrinkling my nose. That should ignite the dynamite. Picking up the water jug, he filled my glass. *Wot* a gentleman eh!

"Water on troubled oils?"

I wasn't quick enough to hide my puzzlement.

"You'll need to think about it. Take your time."

It's confirmed, he did bring out the worst in me.

"And may I ask," valiantly holding onto my patience, "what brings you to this table in particular? If you look around you will see the dining hall is littered with empty places. And you who are so pure in thought," my tongue gabbling on, "wouldn't want to be seen with a known racist. I might put poison in your dinner, for all you know and then you'd have a terrible problem getting out the next issue of *Spanner*. Not to mention that this devil in Asian skin, having got good and rid of you, might take over herself and print her racist rhymes on your tombstone!"

He raised an eyebrow.

Oh God, I'd been practising that for months and still couldn't do it.

"Can I get a word in? Please."

"As many as you like. I've nearly finished my din-dins, and I won't take long over my jam roly-poly. My favourite pudding. Yum yum, I just shovel it down my throat, and let it take the lift straight down to my tummy. No detours on the way..."

"Have you heard about the Asian Beauty Contest?" Suresh interrupted.

"Are you going to be entering?" I asked sweetly, licking the jam off my spoon.

"I wondered if you'd like to write an article about it," completely ignoring my jibe. "You would be completely free to express your opinions."

"And you would be completely free to suppress them? No thank you. Here's mud in your eye," holding up the unmentionable glass of water, drinking it down in loud slurps.

"Look, I also wanted to apologise. Perhaps I wasn't very tactful. But I'm afraid I really didn't like that poem, and I did think it was offensive. But, I assure you, it wasn't meant as any kind of a personal thing."

"Calling me racist, isn't personal! I mean, have you looked at the colour of my skin?" banging my hands down on the table.

"Not much skin colouring, is there?" bringing his hands out and putting them next to mine. "In fact, though it's only a matter of shade, I think I'm actually darker than you."

"Comparing heart lines?" VT's shadow fell over us. And her shadow's shadow. They sat down next to him, smiling their piranha smiles at me. "How are you getting on? Making progress?" asked VT, her meaning clear.

I wondered if she had told him. Had they had a good laugh about it? Perhaps they were playing a game of double bluff, him pretending he didn't know anything about it, getting me to think I was succeeding in winning the silly bet, and at the last minute he would turn against me. I decided to keep as far away from him as the school walls would allow. I certainly wouldn't do any articles.

"Sorry. I have to rush off. Mustn't miss my delousing appointment," hitching my tote bag onto my shoulders and rushing off in such a panic that I crashed into a little first year, returning his tray and crockery. Poor little mite looked as though he'd been hit by a steamroller. Behind me, VT Rice and shadow giggled openly. But Sir Galahad was there in a flash, soothing the little one and helping me pick up all the plates and glasses. I felt like crying with frustration and anger. I couldn't even make a decent exit. Had to trample over everything in sight like some overgrown octopus!

"It's alright. No-one's hurt. Nothing's broken," he was holding my arm.

Good heavens, I was shaking.

"Why don't you sit down for a minute?" pulling forward a chair.

Sit down and say what?

"I'm late for a class. 'Bye. Thanks for your help." I managed to make it out the door without causing any more catastrophes.

I found out about the Beauty Contest. The posters were littered all over our supermarket. A multi-racial Beauty Contest. There would be ten judges, half Asian and half English. The contestants, if you can call them that, half Asian and half English as well. Billed as a unique event, the first ever of its kind. The brain child of some Harmony Committee, half Asian and half English, wouldn't you know it, and half barmy with it I thought. So this is their solution to the racial problems in our town. I could just picture it all. The English voting for the Asians because they think it's working for harmony and the Asians voting for the English because they won't want to be accused of only choosing their own. It'll all end in a draw. The blood-hungry gangs in the town will home in on it, fists will fly, blood will spill and it'll be all-out riot.

I was so upset. I could see it all as clear as though it had already happened. The gangs were just waiting for an excuse to have a battle. The English gangs had always been there but the Asian gangs were fairly recent. It was all supposed to be secret, but of course everyone gossiped and speculated about who was in a particular gang. There were always stories going round about initiation rituals, blood oaths and fights. I didn't believe the half of it.

I cornered Gazzy as she was sharing her lunch with

the ducks.

"Mum sent some gobi ke parathas for you. She said you're the only one who really appreciates her cooking." Then I stopped talking and gave them to her. I should take a vow of silence, that would teach my tongue a lesson. Sometimes I just didn't know what it was saying. It just carried on and on and carried on, carrying me into trouble.

Gazzy said, "Thank you," and put the parathas by her side.

She really exasperated me these days. The old Gazzy would have gobbled them up double quick. I felt like saying to her that if she didn't want them, I wouldn't mind having them myself, but I didn't, remembering my Indian manners. So I showed her the leaflet about the Beauty Contest and told her, all in a laughing and joking way about what I thought was going to happen.

"Do you think I should go to the police with my suspicions?" A wide grin on my face, inviting her to join in and share the humour of this silly scenario. "Can you imagine it? 'Mr Policeman, I have had a vision.' 'Certainly madam, would you care to give us a statement on it. Oi, Oi, hold on, looks like a confession of a felony not yet committed. Off to the cells with her'!"

Gazzy didn't laugh but then what did I expect.

"You might be right. The possibility of violence is always there."

I sat up straight. "These gangs are nothing but hot air. Silly little boys who don't have anything to do. Now if their mothers kept them busy and occupied, doing the hoovering, shopping, cooking, cleaning, they wouldn't have time to get together and play war-games."

"The gangs are there. And they're not very nice."

"How do you know?" What did she know that I didn't?

"Why don't you do that article that Suresh asked you to do?"

"Because, you know why. And how do you know he asked me?"

"News gets around."

"You mean VT's big mouth."

"Well your's isn't any smaller."

This wasn't like the new Gazzy. I looked away from her, whatever she said next was going to hurt.

"You're always judging other people, you talk as though you know everything there is to know. You think you can sail through life with a joke and a quip. That whole thing about shortening your name so it became Hari-jan! You thought it was so cute."

"As I remember, you thought it was not only cute but dead clever. You used it more than I ever did."

"But I don't any more. Or hadn't you noticed?"

"You hardly talk to me, how am I supposed to know? I'm the one who follows you round like a sick little dog and wags my tail like mad when you happen to glance my way."

"But what have you done with your name? Got a few laughs and that's it. You talk about your parents' money like it was dirt. But at least they've got it, and that means you've got it. You'll always be comfortable and secure." She looked away across the pond. The ducks were floating in the water, heads tucked in, feathers fluttering. "Papa's being made redundant. And he's ... well, other things have happened too. Amma's going to have to look for a job. Never worked in her life. She shouldn't have to do that at her age. With her broken English. They'll give her a right old time. I said I'd leave school and work. But Amma wouldn't let me. Education and all that. I decided I'd work myself silly and get the best grades I could. That's the only thing I can do in return and I'm going to do it. What are you going to do? Make bets and turn your back on them?"

"Gazzy!"

"You're floating through life just like those ducks."

"You want I should lay him?" Oooh, that wicked word of Babylon!

"Don't be stupid! He's offering you an olive branch, asking you to do some serious work. How does he know you can write an article. He's taking a risk. And what do you do?"

"Gazzy. I'm keeping my head tucked in. Just like those ducks. But it's because I'm in dangerous waters."

"And who got you there?"

"I know all that!" I was shouting. "But that's why I couldn't. Can't you see?"

"You poor little rich girl. Life is so tough."

"What do you want me to do?"

"I don't want you to do anything. But we're going different ways. I mean I am, you're still stuck where you were a year ago. I don't see any guts in you. You think it was easy for me to come to school in this kind of dress?"

"I wear shalwar kameez too."

"And look at the way you wear it! It'd take a Sherlock Holmes to work out what it's really supposed to be. Another cop out. One look at me and the whole world knows what I am. Or they think they do – stupid, foreign, one of those fanatical Muslims, a dirty Arab. You think it's easy to walk down the street, go into a shop? You think it's easy to go off for my prayers with everyone looking and sniggering?"

"Dear me, I didn't quite realise you were Jhansi Ki Rani and Joan of Arc all rolled into one!"

2
LADIES FINGERS

I decided to put Gazzy, Suresh, and VT Rice in a section of my mind called 'Deep Freeze'. And I was determined to enjoy my weekend. I'm allowed Sunday off. Isn't that generous! Saturdays I'd be chained to the till no matter what. Though that is a situation I wish to change, and am already giving great thought to the strategy, the negotiating points and the campaign. Why didn't I just go and ask? Ha! Why didn't I just go and bang my head against a brick wall! Why didn't I just refuse ... Why didn't I actually?

Because I am child of Asian *Phamily* and I couldn't. Don't ask me why. I don't have the answers. (Like my Authentic Indian Accent? It's not your curry powder stuff. Once Gazzy and I carried it on for weeks and weeks, 'till the teacher-wallahs talked about putting us in remedial class.)

Sunday, I went to see my Masi, my Mum's sister. Mum and Dad dropped me off in the afternoon, on their way to some 'function'. They never go to parties, they 'attend functions'. They watched as I waited at the door, carrying the heavy bags of groceries. What did they think was going to happen? Something from outer space would come and whisk me away?

Masi, my sweet little Masi opened the door and gave me a hug that only reached my chest. That's good enough for me! She was older than my mother and ran a three bedroom house that's cosy and welcoming. We went into the kitchen and without even asking she put on the pan for my favourite Indian chai, talking non-stop about how thin and tired I looked. A shining frying pan was nearby and I picked it up to examine myself. I must have looked haggard, utterly exhausted. The frying pan reflected a plump, chubby face. Perhaps I should go on a diet.

"Your mother should make sure you eat properly. Sandwiches and chips are not proper food. Business is hard work, but everyone works hard and if you don't work hard how do you look after your family? That is true," putting plates of goodies on the table.

Not to look too eager, I started unpacking the bags I'd brought. She'd refused every offer of help my parents made and had only recently stopped protesting about the bags and boxes that my mother was determined to give. A compromise between two strong-willed women.

"Sit, sit. Sit down and eat," taking my arm and pushing me into a chair. "You young people, so restless, so running about."

Bringing the teapot to the table, a fraction of a pause, that only we who knew her so well would notice, a quick glance over at my uncle's picture, before she poured the lovely spicy tea. Their's was an arranged marriage made in Nirvana. It had never bothered her that here, in England, he didn't get the kind of jobs he should have had with his qualifications. What bothered her was that he got cancer and then died. She was always small but I'm dead certain she's got smaller since his death.

"Where's Binny?" I asked, picking up a couple of gulab jamuns. Thin! Masi had said. My whole life revolved around food. All the exciting things happen, don't they, when I'm getting my teeth stuck into something.

"Driving lesson. She wants to pass first time. She has two lessons a week."

My mouth dropped a yard. Two lessons a week! Is Binny getting the bug of ambition?

"She is still at her job with the council. It is a good job. Very much security."

Very much my cousin's idea of life I thought. Binny was alright, and I didn't mind her at all, except she's not the kind you'd describe as bags of fun.

"You know what has happened, Baby?"

I pointedly glared at my Masi. She pointedly ignored me. What a thing to be called at my age! I just can't get her to stop using it.

"Something very strange. I am being promoted."

"Good for you Masiji. You deserve it. Let's celebrate." I helped myself to a samosa.

"After fifteen years. Why? I have never asked for anything. It is a nice place, I like working there. I have friends. But why now? There are others who are much better educated. I asked Mr Johnson, 'Why are you doing this?' He smiled, he took my hand, you know how these English men are. No respect for women. We are talking merely. He does not need to touch me. He tells me all sorts of things, I am very experienced, I am good at dealing with other people...

Me, I didn't even touch my samosa. Sounded like this Mr Johnson fancied my Masi. How dare he! I felt like sorting him out right then.

"I think I will refuse," she said finally.

"Oh, *don't*." I felt so upset. Why should she have to give up promotion just because of some silly man who's got his pants in a twist? Boxes, that's what she'd been making for fifteen years. And not only your tiddly little ones to chuck a bauble in for Christmas, but some real heavy duty stuff. Boxes for car spares, washing machines - the lot. Once, the machine went wrong and started stapling her hand like it was a piece of cardboard. You'd never seen such a mess. She deserved to be promoted. They owed it to her. Yet she only got it when some dirty old man thinks he can get his wicked way with her. "I'll go and see them, find out what's what. You should get your promotion without any funny business going on."

Masi smiled. "Baby, you're not afraid of anything. That's good. But, let's forget this factory business. I have a job for you now. I'll get the atta ready for the purees and you go and buy some bhindi. Don't go to the first shop, I saw their bhindi. Terrible. Left over from last year, I'm sure. There is a new one, two roads away to the left." She'd got her purse and was taking out some money.

There is a first time for everything, and this time I was footing the bill.

"And also go to the video shop and choose something for us to watch. But only if it has my favourite stars in it."

"I know," I said, rolling my eyes in resignation. "Here we go, another evening with Raj Kapoor, Dilip Kumar etc," fanning a yawn. "The mouldy oldies."

"You are a jungly child who knows nothing of *kwality*. Now go," pushing the money into my hands.

"*I vill, I vill*, but this stays here," putting it on the table and dashing out before she could lift a foot to follow and push those pound coins into my pocket.

Everfresh was the new shop and I must say it looked very much like its new name. All green and white and fresh looking, displaying glamorous veggies in gorgeous colours, deliciously perfumed with the smell of fresh dhaniya, methi and mangoes. I calculated the money in my purse and decided I could stretch to two mangoes plus the bhindi. Putting them in the green basket (of course), I joined the group by the bhindi section. They were all going through it like they were searching for gold, heads down in concentration, fingers shifting and searching and choosing. I ain't doing that, I decided, I'd be here all day and miss out on my gup-shup with Masi. Any that don't look too old and mangy got shoved in my paper bag. I thought I was almost done when I heard a voice, a male voice, at my side.

"That one's no good. It'll be too stringy."

I don't turn round to look, because I had a horrible suspicion.

"What you do is," lifting one up to show me, "see if you can snap the pointed end off with a flick of your thumb."

I stared at his fingers, mesmerised. And they do the trick.

"If it snaps off immediately, it's a good one. And then you can comfortably pop it into your bag. Like this," chucking it into mine.

"Hi, Suresh." Well I couldn't keep mum for ever. "Fancy bumping into you. Do you come here often?"

"All the time. My mother burdens me with the family chores." His face was changing all over and this time it was saying let's share a joke. "I should have done all this yesterday. I was supposed to. I meant to do it. But I was busy."

Busy doing what? Busy with whom? None of my business I told myself severely.

"Want some more?" he asked.

35

"No," clutching my bag to myself.

"Sure? They shrivel quite drastically when they're cooked. It's always better to buy more."

"No. I mean, it's enough, for us, for the evening. So nice meeting you. 'Bye. Thanks for your help."

His eyebrow went up again. "Not at all."

I paid my dues and left. Phew! as they say, wiping the sweat from my brow. Oh God it was wet! I must have been sweating buckets. Had he noticed? Better get back to Masi's quick, shut the door and hope nothing else happens. I actually started back, then remembered the video.

Mr Chandra's changed everything round too. It's gone all modern. No sign of the rolls of materials, stainless steel dishes, incense and what-nots that cluttered up every inch. Now it's videos, videos and more videos. I shook my head to clear it. Why couldn't everything stay as it was? How was I supposed to find what I want among all this choice? I went up to the counter, in search of Mr C, the film guru. All I'd have to do is give him a vague description of what I thought my Masi wanted and he'll come up with a sure-fire hit. No sign of Mr C. Instead a horribly handsome young man, dressed in a black suit, looking like something out of the *Godfather*, was busy ringing the till. He hardly looked up as I told him what kind of film I wanted. "Everything's out. Choose what you want," waving his hand airily.

Stupid idiot. I didn't know what I wanted. I sighed and started working my way through the titles. Masses of modern stuff. Even I couldn't bear most of it. All shouting and screeching and fighting. I was about half way through and had three possibles in my hand when I moved to another carousel and came face to face with… Wotsit.

"Fancy bumping into you. Do you come here often?" he asked, a big grin on his face.

I sighed. I just didn't believe this was happening. How many years had I been visiting my Masi? And how come I've never seen hide nor hair of him before?

"Do you live round here?" I asked accusingly.

"Yes. Bodmin Road."

Ah, the road with the big Victorian houses.

"But we're new arrivals. About six months ago."

Well that makes sense.

"You live round here too?"

I didn't bother to correct him. Why bother? Let fate do its dirty work. Twice in one day! And after all my efforts to keep out of his way.

"It's a nice area."

"Most people can't wait to move out. Too many *of our sort.*"

"But I love it. It's really nice round here, mixing in with different people. It's great to be able to go round the corner and buy all your Indian groceries. On a Sunday afternoon too. Before, if we wanted to watch an Indian film we had to drive four miles out here."

"How nice." It sounded really sarky. But I didn't mean it that way. I just didn't know what else to say. I was truly flummoxed.

"Found anything interesting?"

I handed over my selection.

"About average," handing one back, "this one too. B-grade kind of stuff. *Pyaasa*! This is brilliant. I've been wanting to see this one for a long time."

Brilliant huh? Now what do I do? Snatch it out of his hands? Or do sacrifice, satyagraha and offer it to him? Earn some Brownie points with Gazzy. On the other hand it could just make me look like an over-eager bimbo, dying to lick his boots and win the bet. I kept silent. I wouldn't mind offering it to him, but would he understand my noble motives? As it was he'd moved off to the cash till, my film in his hand. What was he playing at? Was this video-thievery? I wasn't going to lower myself to his level and go chasing after him. I dived off to the opposite corner and picked a couple at random, pretending to read their silly little blurbs. Talk about being frazzled - I felt fried to a crisp!

"Here you are," he was back, holding it out to me.

Oh, God he'd gone and paid for it. A true little Indian prince, ain't he! And me? I'm the witch with the evil heart. I pushed it back towards him.

"You've wanted to see it for ages. Do take it."

"You chose it. It's yours," putting it back in my hands.

I pushed it back into his and before we know it we were into one of those Indian scenes of extra super-politeness, the video shuttling between our hands. He'd realised it too because we were both giggling like mad. I tried to stop but I couldn't as he plonked it back in my hands for the umpteenth time. I shoved it straight back, with more force than I intended. He lost his balance, hitting a carousel, sending video covers flying through the air. The 'orribly handsome young man looked at us and pointedly pointed towards the door. Not being slow on the uptake we took the hint and staggered out, leaving a trail of laughter behind us.

Outside, we leant against a shop window, trying to calm down, then bursting into giggles as we looked at the video lying among his veggies. I tried to choke everything back and ended up with loud deep hiccups. Oh Hell! How babyish can you get! He rushed off into a shop and this time I didn't even begin to think of an evil thought before he was back with a can of Coke. I gulped it half down and he watched concerned, as the hiccups eventually got fewer and fewer.

And now it was all quiet between us. In fact, a little frightening, for what do we do now or rather what do I do? I should pick up my bags and go. But I didn't want to. And he wasn't saying anything. Neither was his face, it had settled into a quiet, thinking expression. VT was right. He did do it in a heavy way. I looked away, at the buses, the shops, the people. What would someone else do/say in my place?

"Should we be standing here, like this? What if someone from your family sees us?" he asked and something in my stomach did a turnaround.

What was he about to suggest? What will I do? What will I say?

"My mother's drummed all the traditional ways into me," he said hesitantly, "so what I'm trying to say is, that I know the rules, but…"

"And I know how to break them," said I, fluttering my lashes like a demented bird, biting my tongue too late.

"Really?" looking closely at me.

Well done Hari-jan. You've done it again. "Your bhindis are spilling out," I informed him. The bag had split open. He thought I was taking the mick and meant something I didn't mean. I bent down to pick them up. If he wanted to stand and glare it was up to him. 'Ladies Fingers' as they were called by the English, green and tapering and temperamental, if

39

they weren't prepared just right they'd seep out their gluey gunge and ruin your cooking. He was down on the ground too, his fingers occasionally brushing against mine as we quickly chucked them back in the bag. His face, eyes, hair too close for comfort.

We stood up and he held out the tape to me. This time I took it. "Have a nice evening," he said, turning to go.

So that was it. An unexpected encounter of the disappointing kind. I didn't even know what I had expected though. In actual fact, things being as they were, I had no right to expect anything. On top of which I had to go acting like a cheap little tart. All my fault. So why did I feel so empty?

Dying to say something, terrified of messing it up, VT Rice and the bet all congealed inside me, I'd only got a second left before he'd be off and away. "I'll do the article, on the Beauty Contest," I blurted out, out of breath. Though why I should be out of breath I don't know.

He stood still, stunned. "Very good. That will be good," he said repeating himself.

"Do you want to come to my Masi's house?"

I'd really taken leave of my senses. Who's to say I wouldn't get lynched?

"Your Masi?"

"That means my mother's..."

"I know what it means. I can't. It's impossible. I have to do the cooking. I've already missed two turns. My mother will lynch me if I don't do it tonight."

Oh well, that's two of us saved from a lynching.

"Does your Masi live round here?"

"Yes, just a couple of roads down. I'm visiting her."

"I thought you lived round here."

"I lied."

"Why?"

"Because…," I trailed off. What should I say to him, and how much did he know? What if he knew everything? There's a song my aunt plays, called *Suspicious Minds*. That's me. "Because it's too complicated." I finished quickly.

"Why?"

Does he always repeat himself?

"Because…" desperately thinking, "I'm an Indian girl, you're an Indian boy and there are certain rules, as you know already, that can't be broken." Well done! I congratulated myself. When at a loss fall back on tradition! It may take you out of the frying pan and chuck you into the fire, but that's another problem.

"You said you knew how to break the rules."

Doesn't he ever forget anything? Can't he see a joke when he hears one?

"I lied." This time I was smug. How could he be so stupid?

"Why?"

Relentless interrogation. Where did he think he was? *LA Law*? "Because I wanted you to think I'm a super smart streetwise city girl."

"You're very good on alliteration. Why did you want me to think that?"

I glared at him. Did I have to spell out the obvious? Hadn't I done enough? He smiled back at me. I heard *filmi* music in the air.

"Harjinder, Harjinder." My cousin Binny was tugging at my arm, an open car door behind her, Indian music blaring out, *Sita's Driving School* written on the side.

"I saw you when we stopped at the traffic lights.

41

Hang on a moment I'll get my things."

She looked so different – hair short and henna-streaked, wearing a tight black skirt with a very chic blazer.

I wanted to shriek my amazement, then remembered I was in company. This wasn't my cousin Binny who was into flowered blouses and pleated skirts. This was a trendy alien who had taken over her body.

"OK. Got everything."

Everything included a carrier bag from an expensive boutique plus a bunch of flowers. Flowers? We've never squandered a penny on a petal in all our lives!

The car drove off. She stood smiling, waiting for an introduction. I mumbled their names, waving my hand between them. Suresh came out with all the right 'intro' phrases, even added a couple of funny sentences about how we got thrown out of the video shop. Then made his excuses, said goodbye and went. Just like that!

Binny was bubbling, "He's so nice. Very polished. Did I interrupt something?"

Of course she had, the idiot.

"He's your dark secret, is he?" digging me in the ribs.

"Ouch! And no, he isn't. I hardly know him," I protested. She wasn't going to believe a word I said. That was obvious. Is this how things happen in life? An accidental meeting gets turned into something that it isn't. Everyone gossips about it, then those two people are lumbered with something that doesn't even exist, although they may want it to happen, at least one of them may want it, but if it hasn't happened and yet everyone thinks its

42

happened... I stopped thinking. This was too difficult for me. I'd have to talk it out with Gazzy. Binny's said something about a man. She wasn't still going on about Suresh, was she?

"He's changed my whole life. I was only half living before. I didn't know about good clothes, I never thought about getting ahead in life..."

I was astounded. What on earth was she saying? What man? Who? Did my Masi know? Was she (dreaded words) getting up to no good! My shock, astonishment, everything must have showed on my face, because she just laughed and laughed.

"You should see yourself. You look as though you've been hit by a sledgehammer."

"I have. What's going on?"

"You haven't been listening. You're so self-centred, Harjinder. I've been pouring out my heart to you and you haven't heard a single word. Still thinking about 'your young man' eh?"

She said it so coyly, I could've thumped her. I was suffering from complete nervous exhaustion. I'll never go out for bhindi and video again, I vowed to myself.

"Now listen, this is important," said Binny, shaking my arm. "He works at Marks and Sparks. That's where I saw him. He's so beautiful 'Jindi," eyes went misty and gooey.

Beautiful! A man?

"Looks just like Nehru. Patrician good looks. That's what they're called. Ros, who's tutoring me for my English 'A' levels told me that. I took her along to see him."

"Didn't know you were doing exams," I muttered, rubbing my arm and grumbling, she'd been keeping secrets, secret from me.

"I've got to. I've got to be a credit to him. After all he's a trainee manager there."

"Oh, so he thinks you're not good enough for him. Sounds like a real creep."

"Silly. He doesn't know anything about it. He doesn't even know me yet. We're nearly home, I'll tell you quick, but you're not to say a word to anyone."

Cor Blimey! You gotta give it to us Indians. We're really something. Binny hadn't even spoken to him and yet she was behaving like they're already engaged. It was love at first sight, on her part, in between the desserts and the delicatessen. And like a good Indian girl she came home and told her Mum.

"You know how Mummy goes on about *kwality*, especially Marks and Spencer's *kwality*, She even buys our loo paper from there because the *kwality* is so good. I thought she might be angry about me having chosen a man by myself and falling in love with him before marriage, you know how old fashioned she is."

Yes, I knew. I could understand this last bit, though I know many a one who wouldn't.

If you're heading for an arranged marriage then you should arrange yourself not to fall in love with anyone before the event.

"So I said to her, 'I've found the man you'll want me to marry, Mummy, and I know you'll want me to marry him because he's got that something special – he's got Marks and Spencer's *kwality*,'" chuckled Binny, ending her story with a triumphant smile.

I sighed. Masi's house wasn't far away. I could see the door. I could see myself collapsing in a chair and never getting up again.

"What if he's married, Binny?"

"He doesn't wear a wedding ring. I've looked."

"He might be engaged."

"Mummy's doing her detective work. If he is, then she'll find out."

"He might have a girlfriend, that she may not find out."

"Don't be so horrible 'Jindi, don't you want me to be happy?"

"Yes. That's why I'm asking all these questions."

Binny turned round to face me, her door keys in her hand. "Mummy's doing everything through her network, the way they do it. Your parents are in on it too. Don't you think they haven't thought of these things? These people are smarter than you think, and," waving the keys at me like a 'bunch of fives', "you tell me which other way guarantees happiness."

Guarantees of happiness? Depends on the time period don't it? Twelve hours? You got it, no problem. Twelve Days? Stretching it a bit. Twelve years? No way. But I couldn't let it drop. "Even if all the other things are alright, he may say 'no', Binny."

Binny shook her head, as she opened the door, "'Jindi, you're such a bore."

Don't things have a funny way of turning around - I used to say that to her!

"I'll take the risk. He's worth the risk. Isn't your's worth a risk?"

"He's not mine, he's got a girlfriend, and," I continued quickly, before the expression on her face drowned me in sympathy, "I don't care about him, at all." That's true isn't it? "But I did take a risk today," announcing it like I'd done a good deed.

Now I was stuck with the Beauty Contest, burdened with the problems of dealing with my parents' objections to time off work for my journalistic career. Plus all the aggro I'd get from them about going out, plus, I didn't know a damn thing about him and what he thought about me. And plus, I didn't know how much he knew, and plus, I'd got a tense nervous headache.

Masi gave me two aspirins, a big orange shawl to wrap around my shoulders and switched on the video. He was right. It was a brilliant film, utterly harrowing, to put it in a couple of lines, it's about a down-and-out poet, whose poems become best-sellers after his (supposed) death. The money rolls in, his friends and brothers get a cut of the percentage, everyone's as happy as bees in a honeypot. Until he turns up again, and they deny him, just like Peter denied Jesus, branding Him an imposter!

I fell asleep thinking about treachery and evil all around me.

3
CRIME AND PUNISHMENT

I thought I'd better get some more information from His Majesty about the Beauty Contest, which I now thought of as the *Beastly Contest*, before facing my parents' third degree interrogation on it. The How? What? Why? Where? Who?

I'd be in the dock and they'd be judge and jury, presuming me guilty of traitorous motives and desires before I'd even had a chance to flirt with the 'Devil of Temptation.'

Sound strange to you? It's perfectly logical to me. It's all about motives, you see. Ever noticed how every TV detective will be hunting for the M O T I V E ... 'Aaagh...' *croaked the dying villain, 'how did you guess it was me that killed the baron, set fire to the Rolls, stole the jewels and ran off with the butler?' 'Simple...' said the detective, trying to rub a stain off his mac. 'Revenge was the motive driving you to these dastardly acts, revenge for the time when the baron kept smashing into your car at the dodgems...'*

It was break time. I skittered through the corridor, intent on my urgent mission. As I skilfully wove my way through the human traffic, I glimpsed two stupid yobos, peering in through a door window, giggling and making funny little gestures with their hands. It wouldn't take a brainless idiot to work out what was going on. They were on their knees by the time I reached them, mumbling mumbo-jumbo in-between their stupid cackles. And they weren't doing it quietly, like it was a joke just for them, they meant to be loud and meant Gazzy to hear them, not to mention the growing and appreciative crowd around them.

I grabbed them by their silly little heads, banging them into each other, twisting tufts of hair under my hands, kicking any leg that tried to straighten and stand up. I don't know what I was saying, but I could have slaughtered them. Now I know what blind rage means.

"Stop it. Stop it!"

I heard it the second time.

"Let them go," shouted Gazzy standing in front of us. "Let them go Hari. It doesn't matter."

Who made her the Guardian Angel of Mercy? I shook my head. I couldn't trust myself to speak. I started dragging them off. Away from Gazzy who'd make me give them up. I wanted them punished. The gathered crowd were egging me on now, having completely switched loyalties, showering me with suggestions about suitable punishments. Bloodthirsty lot!

"Hari, let them go or I'll…" and there was a pause, "I'll do something."

I stopped. This was something new. What would she do? I started dragging them off just to find out. Harder this time, because by now they were almost on their feet. But my height kept them under control, for the moment.

Gazzy got in front of me, putting out her arms and blocking my way. It was hard enough dragging two struggling and twisting baboons, without having to manoeuvre around her as well. If there is treachery in the world, I thought, then this was it. I dropped them, not before giving a final kick. The crowd booed their dissatisfaction and disappointment.

"Not so fast," said Gazzy, as the two yobs were about to turn tail and run, "I'd like to talk to you."

Oh my God, talk! As though they had a brain somewhere in those racist little heads.

I walked off fast, my mind switching to autopilot and my guts saying I never wanted to see Gazzy again and my eyes streaming with tears. Without realising it, I'd reached the cupboard the magazine-wallahs called their office. I couldn't go in there in this state. I sat on the steps, wiping myself dry on my sleeve, scrubbing my face to remove the tearstains. I had to hurry or I'd be late for lessons. I'd half decided not to bother with Suresh and leave it for another time, when something hit my spine. I was sent tumbling to the floor and a granite boulder of a body landed full smack on me, flailing hands grabbing for my hair.

Oh Fate, as they would say in a Greek tragedy, Thy revenge is as swift as it is just. VT Rice it was, massaging her ankles and staring crossly at me. I picked myself up off the floor, hoping something was irreparably broken, so I could go home and not ever have to come back to school. Suresh and his sidekick, Jamie, nearly repeated the collision as they jostled through the door to find out what had happened, full of anxious concern and exclamations.

"There is a door. You could have come through and said hello to us," complained VT.

"I was sorting out my inner soul and so couldn't knock on heaven's door."

They looked completely blank. Who wouldn't!

"Are you alright? Anything hurt? Come inside, have a coffee," Suresh dished out sympathy with the invite, as he helped me up. VT didn't miss a thing.

"Would anyone like to know if I've broken my ankle?" she inquired querulously.

"Veronica, have you broken your ankle?" asked Jamie, helping her up and through the door into the office.

"Why were you sitting on the steps?" VT demanded.

I was feeling so broken up inside, I knew if she asked me a second time I'd burst into tears.

"I'd love a coffee," I declared brightly, getting some more coffee drinking practice in. "No-one else can boast such luxuries in this school."

As Suresh was sorting out the kettle and mugs, VT helped herself to the only comfortable chair. I stood around like a spare part, feeling bruised and battered, emotionally and physically. Jamie brought a chair over for me, which was nice of him. He really was startling close to, having pure blonde hair and bright blue eyes.

VT must have been on her way out when she decided to do me some GBH. Fair's fair and I was being unfair. How was she to know I was sitting on the steps mopping up my woes? She could have looked.

Anyway, if she was on her way out, what was she doing back here? Honestly I'm so useless in emergencies. I should have realised that if I was here, then she'd slither back in here too. I should have done the opposite and run back to class. What a first class idiot I am! Now I was going to be late and an object of wrath for Mrs Parfitt.

Suresh handed me a mug of hot coffee, with a reassuring smile, which did nothing to reassure me. I had come bouncing along planning to use the article as the reason for my visit, and perfectly true it was, but it was the hidden motive – (see! It reared its ugly head again. Motives, hissed Harjinder-Vader, is the *force* that makes the Universe turn and turn againnnnn) - that VT was sniffing out. And she was on the right track too, except that it was nothing to do with the bet.

I'd wanted to see that So-and-So again. So there, I admit it! He hadn't invited me, he hadn't come chasing after me. I'd done all that, and lost Gazzy along the way. Correction. This time she'd lost me, thrown me away.

Mr Almighty sat stirring his coffee, completely unaware of the drama around him. Or was he?

"Do you think we're the same shoe size?" asked VT pretending innocence, eyeing my Reeboks.

"You do have rather dwarf feet, but I'm sure you'll manage to hobble around in them."

"I doubt I'll ever need to. I've sent off for a book on elocution."

I needed a shield. I couldn't duel with her today. Asking for pen and paper, I butted into Suresh's conversation with Jamie about the next issue. I tuned myself up to be brisk and business-like and started putting my questions, explaining my need to have as much information as possible.

"Since you have been brought up, so very traditionally," I stressed, trying to ignore VT's sly smile, "you know how difficult it will be for me to get my parents' permission."

She folded her arms and listened intently. I needed to know how long it might take, who I should see, why I would need to see them...

"Seems to me you need a chaperone," sneered Madame. "That would make it much easier to convince your parents."

I could just see her volunteering for the job.

"Why don't you ask Suresh to guard you as you go on your dangerous mission? That way Mummy and Daddy need never have a qualm. Carry a mobile telephone with you, that way they can check up on you whenever they feel like it."

"It's not a joke, Veronica. Negotiating with parents is a delicate business," reprimanded Suresh, "and I would be seen as part of the enemy, not part of the chaperone pack. You know very well how I have to explain everything to my parents."

"We know," she sighed. "We know, we have much experience of being the go-bet..."

"Veronica!" he said warningly.

Her arms were folded, her eyes narrowed. Were the golden couple about to have a tiff? Time to make a move. I'd had my fill of aggro for the day.

"Let me know how things go," Suresh came to open the door. "Don't let it beat you, we'll work something out."

He was just too good to be true. He couldn't be real, it's an elaborate facade.

"OK, will do Doc. By the way, the film was stupendous," I flicked an eye towards VT. She could make whatever she liked of it. "It was really amazing."

"I'll come with you," said VT jumping up on her supposedly injured ankle.

Our's is a large sprawly school, lots of new buildings tacked onto the original Victorian one in the middle, and many a walk has to be taken before you reach your lessons.

"How's it going?" asked VT, as soon as we were out of earshout.

"The economy's still in a terrible state. The

recession is biting very deeply, more businesses going bust…"

"Look, I know shopkeeping is your trade, but get the cash-till off your mind for a moment and think back to a bet we made. Is it still on or not?"

Oh God, why isn't there a God to whisk me away when I needed one? I should be honest with her, but I couldn't. I'd feel small and inferior like a coward who throws in the towel before the fight has even begun. And half the school saw me lose out to Gazzy. If I said yes, it would be like making the bet all over again, and there'd be no room for excuses no more.

"VT… Ooops! Confusing you with a friend of mine. Veronica, um, do you really want to put yourself in danger of losing him? You seem so happy together."

She laughed. She had a very nice laugh, you know how very few people have lovely smiles, VT to be fair to her, had this lovely musical laugh.

"Trying to cry off?"

"No!" I said indignantly, then stood stock still, knowing my fate was sealed. That 'No' meant 'Yes', the bet was still on.

"I'll give you 'till Diwali. That's two months away. A little less actually, but that won't matter to you. You've already got it sewn up, haven't you? His parents always throw a big Diwali party. Let's see which one of us is there on that night. And don't try to wriggle out of it," wagging her finger at me, "by just getting an invite. Whichever one of us is there, has to be there because she's Suresh's girlfriend. In full view of everyone."

"My parents will kill me. I can't have boyfriends." I was horrified.

"Should have thought of that before, shouldn't you!"

I could stick a thousand pins in her.

"Alright. Diwali it is." She was on. This was war.

Gazzy was waiting for me, when I went to the cloakroom to fetch my coat. I didn't speak to her, I gave her a look that was supposed to speak volumes and marched out, my coat flapping behind me. She caught me up by the school gate, inviting me home for tea. This was a big honour. It's been a very long time since she last invited me back home. I nodded.

Gazzy's house was a small two bedroomed place in a row of houses that were all the same. Some were decked out with heavy ornamentation, lamps, stone cladding, elongated porches, titchy ponds, frilly frilled curtains. All aspiring and upwardly mobile, except that houses can't go nowhere.

The throbbing sound of the machine seeped out even before we were at the garden gate, and as Gazzy opened the door, its vibrations came through the floorboards and into our feet.

When Gazzy's Mum, who's always been Aunt Fahmida, saw me, she switched off the monster and came forward to give me a big hug and kiss. She's a plump round woman with a broad face. I always wondered how she and her husband, who's not exactly the Handsome Hero type, could have produced Gazzy. Just then Gazzy's Dad came down the stairs, arms full of stitched clothes, saying he'd finished ironing them. Then stood still, seeing me, his embarrassment visible all over him. Aunt Fahmida took the clothes from him and gently persuaded him into a chair. Gazzy grabbed me and pulled me into the kitchen.

"Now you know," she hissed, picking up onions

and began to chop them.

"Know what?"

She looked at me in pure exasperation. "For someone who's so brainy I don't know how you can be so dumb."

There was nowhere to sit in this two-by-two kitchen so I wriggled myself into a corner. Gazzy shoved some garlic and ginger into my hands.

"Make yourself useful. Over here."

Did she love having a slave or did she not? I stood next to her peeling the fiddly stuff. Next door the sewing machine started up again.

She glanced towards the closed door then back at me. "Papa's given up."

"What?"

"Given us up."

"Pardon?"

"Renounced us."

"What?" I sounded dumb even to myself.

"Re… let us go, I mean let go of us."

"He's chucking you out!"

"Relinquished… I'm going to throw the fuck…" she stopped herself just in time, "the dictionary at you." Gazzy sighed.

I must say, privately of course, that I was quite glad to see a spark of the old Gazzy come bubbling up.

"You know what it is, Gaz, it's this Angrezi we got to talk in all the time, 'cos we didn't learn our own lingos properly. Seems to me there are some things you just can't say in Angrezi." Mum said that to me! I've suddenly realized what she was getting at. "There are some things you can't say in English 'cos it just doesn't have the words for them. Savvy!"

She chucked the onions into a pan, then started slicing up some meat.

"Languages have different ideas, meanings, 'cos people live differently, look we're a very... very complex... complicated society..." wish I had a dictionary handy, raising my voice, letting on that the punchline was coming, "so if English doesn't have the same ideas as us, then it doesn't have the words for it. Geddit?"

She looked at me and carried on stirring. "Perhaps that's why I can't understand what you're saying," which left me feeling sheepish. "Done the garlic yet?"

I eagerly shoved it towards her.

"Ginger?"

You bet! I got onto it rightaway.

Gazzy was quiet for a long time. "I'll explain it all, then perhaps you'll understand."

I nodded quickly, I was dead eager to understand.

"Papa lost his job. Happens to lots of people. But what really happened was that he went into business with someone, they bought a shop, just like your Mum and Dad did. He put all his savings in because it seems like, all the Asians buy shops and all the Asians make money. But it didn't work. I don't know why. Uncle Karim kept it open all the time. They had to, to try and make some money. Papa would go off to it, as soon as he got home from work." As she stirred, the steam from the pan clouded her face. "In the end they had to close and sell." Gazzy put the lid on tight and turned the gas down low.

"After a while he called together our relations and a couple of the Mullahs and made a speech. Told them what he'd decided." Gazzy's eyes looked down at the floor, her voice a little trembly. "He told them what had happened, and that he had no money for my dowry, and no money to look after us, and in fact debts to pay off. And because he'd failed in his responsibility, we needn't have any responsibility for him, and I didn't have to do anything for him, or do any of the things I was supposed to… it was dreadful, I cried through it all," blowing her nose on a tissue.

"Then what happened?"

"Nothing really. Everyone told him it wasn't necessary for him to feel so bad, or to say such things, and he should be glad that he's got a family. They said all sorts of things, these things happen to people and they'd all get together and help out. What was quite funny," hiding her face in the steam from the pan again, "my cousin, the chemist one, said in his *purrfect* English accent, 'Uncleji, this is a time of recession, everyone is under stress, you are just over-reacting.' Over-reacting! Honestly Hari, I was crying and laughing at the same time. As if Papa would know what that means. If Papa was English, they'd say he's an eccentric, and bas that would be that."

"An ethnic eccentric!"

That got a smile out of her. "There was all that, but he meant it. Told me so, afterwards, again that I was responsible for myself." Gazzy put some atta in a bowl and started kneading the dough for rotis. "But it got me thinking, if I was free, what did I want to do with myself? What did I want to be? What is my life going to be about?"

"Serious stuff yaar!" I was being flippant, but a huge anger was building up in me. She'd kept all this turmoil, agony and pain secret from me. Why? What did she think I was? She's told me already. I remembered the scene by the duck pond.

"Papa means what he means. Nobody believes

him. But I do. I know him. You see, whatever I did from then on, I was alone, no restrictions, no rules, no conditions, I had to make my own. And everything I did from then on would... matter... it would... have an effect... I would become whatever I did. Do you see what I mean?"

I shook my head. She carried on kneading the dough.

"I wasn't sure, still feel I don't really know. But what I decided, and if you snigger," threatened Gazzy looking sternly at me, "I'm going to throw this atta at you, though it's a sin to waste food."

I put my hands over my mouth, I wouldn't even twitch.

"I decided I wanted to do GOOD in my life," she watched me, "I could have decided I wanted to be RICH, or FAMOUS. I've realised, you have to decide what you want to do and start working at it. Nothing happens automatically. Everything has its own..." tapping her fingers on the bowl trying to think of the right word, "its own..."

"Price?" I ventured to suggest. Having watched umpteen movies in which the villain says... I don't need to say it, you already know.

"Sort of, but not quite, has its own... route, chart, map," looking at me to check if it made sense. "That's why I'm wearing the Hijaab and Jubba, I needed something to strengthen me, help me. There's a lot of wisdom in the Koran, and the Bible, lots of ideas. And praying makes me feel peaceful, strong." She put the atta away in the fridge. "I'm going to sort out those two boys, the ones you were mauling and kicking. But I'm doing it *my* way."

I wasn't angry about that any more, but I was still angry. "You could have told me all this sooner, we've spent half our lives together. You may think I'm an empty headed fool, that I'm not learning, changing and what-not. But what does friendship mean to you in this new life? What have you done for our friendship? I was so angry with you today, you made me look an idiot in front of that whole crowd." My voice was rising, I paused, taking control of myself. "But I can take it, from you. Perhaps my parents could have helped, when your Dad's business was going down. Why didn't you ever talk about it? Why didn't you ask them? They love you."

"Because they're successful," looking at me very hard and straight, "they're good at it, and I couldn't go to them and shop on Papa, and say he's a failure."

"They wouldn't have thought that," I stamped my foot, wanting to scream at her.

"But I would."

"That's stupid."

Next door the sewing machine stopped its thundering. I went quiet. Auntiji came through the door, saying dinner could be early.

"What time did you tell your mother you would be home, Beti?"

Gazzy and I looked at each other in horror. I hadn't phoned home. They'd be sending out search parties by now

"Can I use the phone?" I said, and then I tell you I could've bitten off my tongue there and then.

"Phone on the corner," said Gazzy grabbing her coat. "Let's go."

4
BEAUTY AND THE BEAST

My mother wanted to phone his mother, to check on character, credentials and family history. "I'm not marrying him for God's sake Mum, he's only the editor and I only see him occasionally." This was so embarrassing, I wanted to go and jump into a ditch, I wanted to die. She was leafing through the directory.

"Do not be blasphemous, Harjinder."

"Jesus Christ!" How can she ring up a perfect stranger and start asking her personal questions about her son, all because her daughter wanted to write a teeny-weeny article for the school mag!

"I am warning you, you are going too far!" shaking her nail varnished finger at me. "Jesus Christ was a great Guru. You know there is a theory about His missing years," still leafing through the directory. "Between the ages of... I forget precisely... but before He started His preaching, there are several years of His life missing. It is believed that He spent those missing years in India."

I listened eagerly, letting her know she had all my attention. If she went on long enough perhaps she would forget about her silly phone call.

"Learning the philosophies, the Vedas, everything. There are many similarities between the things He said and our old ideas. For example, when He talks about life after death, what He really means is reincarnation. Everyday now, people believe this, there are many who talk about memories of other lives. What is it our Sadhus do? They give up family ties, they live on charity, that is what Jesus Christ did. He was a great Sadhu. A Mahatma."

She closed the directory with a sigh, I crossed my fingers in hope.

"I can find no number in here for Richardson on that Bodmin Road. I'll ask Vimla to find out," picking up the phone.

I left her to it, I went up to my bedroom, I closed the curtains and sat in the dark. No hope left.

If you think of Beatie, the know-all who's always on the phone, then imagine someone who's even better, that's Aunty Vimla. She knew everything about everyone, and if she didn't know she could find out. Forget about your MI5, CID and phone-tapping. She was more efficient than any of them.

Downstairs Mum was yakking away on the phone. I switched on my Amstrad PCW8512. Sounds grand, don't it? The only thing is, I think Dad got it dead cheap, probably thrown in as a freebie when he bought in his new computer system for the business. I decided I'd do the article as a kind of fly-on-the-wall thing: 'Braving the oceans of lotions, the lakes of lipstick, the masses of mascara, the potions of perfumes, your reporter talks to the B-E-A-U-T-Y W-A-L-L-A-H-S...'

Mum was thundering up the stairs. It must be Emergency Situation Top Priority!! Who was hurt? Who had died? I dashed out onto the landing.

She'd got my Reeboks in her hand.

"Put them on quick, meet me in the car."

This had to be something dire. Outside shoes were never allowed upstairs in our house. They were taken off in the porch and put on in the porch. Outside dirt stayed outside. I dashed out to the front, into the car and away we went! Real Action Woman stuff. "What's happened, Mum, what's happened? Who's hurt? Is Dad OK?"

She looked at me, real puzzled like. "No-one hurt. Everyone alright," but still drove fast.

"Binty's having her baby! Yippee, I'll be an aunt at last."

"Binty is only five months pregnant, too early for baby. We are going to see your friend's mother."

I clutched my head in my hands and groaned with despair. Where would it end? Will she want to inspect his grandparents too? "Look Mummyji," I said, folding my hands in true filmic style, "forgive me please, I no longer want to do magazine article, I want to stay at home and be good Indian girl. Please turn car round. I touch your feet."

She looked at me and giggled.

I must say it was a desirable residence, huge bay windows, a neat little front garden, magnolia tree flowering in the middle. I refused to get out, I folded my arms and stayed put. My mother looked at me, giving a final chuckle and opened the door. Someone must have been watching out for us, because a woman came flying down the steps. I know it sounds all airy-fairy but she ran so quickly, her skirt fanning out behind her, it really did look like she was flying. Then I saw Mum running too, and in another second they were in each others' arms.

I should've guessed, shouldn't I? Give two Indians half a minute to talk to each other and they'll soon work out they're related, even if it's twenty generations removed. Still with their arms around each other, the two women came towards the car. "So this is Harjinder," said the other woman, peering through the window. She had long flowing hair too, though not curly like my Mum's. Perhaps they did have family traits in common. Opening the door, she gently took my arm and helped me out.

"Can you believe it?" She was talking to my Mum, though holding on to me. "We have these big grown up children. Impossible, hain?" both smiling and shaking their heads.

We were led into a huge kitchen at the back, it must have been two or three rooms knocked into one. Mum and Aunty Laxmi, as she introduced herself, were digging up the past, recounting the present, as they talked in that lovely mix of Hindi, Panjabi and English. They were so happy to see each other, even I could feel it. I relaxed, shedding my tension and fear like a snake shedding its skin, and just sat back and listened.

Twenty-five years ago in India, they had been students together. They had graduated, gone their separate ways and lost touch.

"Remember Poonum? The shorty with the spotty face?" Aunty Laxmi talked very fast. "Wanted to marry a boy in the IFS. It happened, she did it. Husband's a diplomat. She's in America now. In fact, David is staying with them. He's over there for a lecture tour. And let me see, who else? Chandra, I bumped into her last time I was in Delhi. Doing OK. Housewife, married to a doctor. She's a disappointment to me. I can't understand her, she hasn't done anything with her life. She's had three children though," fingers tapping the table in puzzlement. "But, Zhara Mara, now there's a surprise! Divorced and dating a film star. We met at a party in Bombay, to launch David's book. At first she pretended not to know me. She's so changed, yaar, you wouldn't believe it. Remember, she's the one refused to go swimming because she'd have to wear a swimsuit and 'it is not becoming in our traditions.'"

"She's such a fatty. Cover story Laxmi, bilkul hogwash!"

"Not any more. Dresses to kill, yaar. Outright homicide. And guess who else I met and where? Zurich! We were sitting in a cafe and a Sardar walks in, and guess who the Sardar was?"

"What about Reita, did she keep in touch with anyone?" Mum wasn't interested in the Sardar.

"Yes, yes, yes, I get news of her. Married into the army. Some colonel, general or whatever. She was that type."

"Don't any of you have ordinary lives?" I asked, tentatively butting in. They were so matter of fact about diplomats, colonels, film stars. I was boggled.

"Of course not, my dear," they both preened. "We were the *Malai de la Malai.*"

I opened my mouth to question and exclaim, that is I was about to say, "What?" and utterly embarrass myself when it dawned upon me. Some God up there must have been looking out for me. Creme de la Creme of course! Idiot.

"You cut off from everyone," Aunty Laxmi accused my Mum. "I heard the gossip, that you'd gone abroad to get married, and khatum! No more news."

"There wasn't time for more. I agreed to get married here, so that I could be near my sister. You remember her? She's two years older than me, but she's a gentle soul. I could never trust her to look after herself." Mum laughed rather sheepishly. "Marriage, children, housework, business. They put my student days very far behind, as though it was another life. I had the children very quickly, and we wanted to make something of our lives, opened a shop and so on. I was lucky if I managed to get a cup of tea. Life here is very hard, Laxmi. There's no-one to help you. And Indians here are becoming very westernised, the sense of... of... belonging to each other, of helping each other has gone."

"And I had no idea you were at school with Suresh," exclaimed Aunty Laxmi, coming over to me giving me a hug. She reminded me of a model, tall and thin, wearing chunky Indian jewellery, broad heavy bangles on her arms. "And if your Mummy hadn't phoned we would never have known we were living in the same town!"

I smiled weakly.

"You know Resham, I think I have been to your supermarket, but only once. You see we have only recently moved here, before we lived out a bit. I always knew you would do business ..."

"You accused me of it often enough ..."

"See how right I was? We were born into the wrong families, you should have been born into mine, you and my father working together – pure synergy! Head of international conglomerate, that's where you would be by now, your stiletto heel digging into the necks of the workers."

"Bukwaas!"

"That's khadi." She saw me looking at her skirt. "I only wear khadi. Listen to this, Resham. When I wanted to marry David the family were not happy, you can imagine..."

She had lovely hand gestures, I found her fascinating. I don't think I'd ever met an Indian woman like her.

"They said many things – it would not last, he will divorce you, the English do not have our values, do not have our sense of responsibility. After six months he will fall in love with someone else and leave you, and so forth and so forth. But one thing which my younger brother said made me most angry, this came into the red-hot volcano category, remember Arjun?"

Mum nodded.

"Yes? Big computer man now, but stupid, always stupid, he started calling me Mrs Memsahib, and taunting me with silly old English songs. Then one day, silly twit, he must have cooked it up with my brothers because they were all sniggering, he put a knife and fork by my plate: 'Mrs Memsahib eat her roti with knife and fork, Mrs Memsahib gobble up rice with silver spoon.' I threw the lot at them and wouldn't have cared if one of them had been mortally wounded. So I vowed I would always wear khadi as my...as my...as a way of showing that I will not become foreign. So I got married in khadi. Resham, you cannot imagine the scandal!" laughing gleefully. "The scandal wasn't that I was marrying out, but that I was getting married in khadi. Chachaji threatened to walk out on the wedding. My family are business people, weddings are big showcase occasions. It is alright to wear khadi to Independence Day celebrations, it is alright for politicos and so on. But for us, money-makers, making a big splash, that's my family's way of being Indian. My way is different. I've made sure that Suresh speaks fluent Hindi and he can read and write it, which is more than can be said for half the Indian children that I meet here. He's perfectly at home in India...Oh good."

Suresh and Miss Veronica VT Rice walked in through the door.

I don't know which of them looked more shocked

to see me ensconced so comfortably in the family kitchen. Aunty Laxmi took Suresh over to my Mum, for introduction and inspection.

"Smart work," whispered VT Rice.

"Thank you."

Mum and Aunty Laxmi were having a tussle, I watched and listened with interest. Who was going to be the winner of this heavyweight contest of female wills?

"Of course you stay for dinner, we haven't met for twenty-five years and you're running out on me in twenty minutes! Ring your husband and tell him where to come."

"Acha, if you insist," sighed my Mum.

I just shake my head in disbelief.

VT and Suresh went out. All I had from him was a 'Hi'. Aren't I lucky! Why don't I just call myself fly-on-the-wall? I thought. Mum and Aunty Laxmi got busy washing, chopping and chatting. My Mother, obviously realising I was feeling left out, plonked garlic and ginger in front of me to peel. That's exactly what Gazzy gave me to do!

Suresh came back in and deigned to recognise my existence, sitting down to help me with my chore in life. He told me, quite unnecessarily, I thought, that Veronica had wanted to borrow some videos, but now she'd gone. Oh really? Then whose ghost was that sitting between us, I wondered. He asked what I thought of the *Mahabharat* that's been showing on TV. Before I could reply, his mother bustled over to us, scooped everything up and shooed us out.

"You bachas go and talk about the burning issues of the world somewhere else...we've got old gossip to catch up on."

"I'm at the top," he said out in the hallway, "three

flights. Better than a workout. Would you like to watch my film? I made it last time I was in India. We go every year, but I've decided, with my cousin Sheetal, that this time we're going to rebel and go see some other part of the world."

He had a huge loft-like space at the top – shelves and shelves of books, paintings, music gear, TV and even a mini-kitchenette. I was livid green with envy. I thought I was well set-up, but he was a hundred points up on me.

"There's no bed!" I exclaimed and immediately blushed.

He wouldn't even be polite and pretend he hadn't noticed, just looked at me grinning, hands in his pockets. Well I wasn't going to look away.

"My bed is downstairs in my bedroom, this is my..." waving his hand out, I bet he's going to say boudoir, I thought, feeling superior, "...nukurdh."

I nodded knowingly (and internally, gave high speed commands to my computer brain to work out what it means double quick!).

"I've got a few episodes of *Nukurdh*, it's a programme on Indian TV. We can have a look at those too if you want, I tape masses of stuff when I go there. Want to watch my film?" going over to his video collection. "I'm the producer, director and writer, the totally forgettable stars are my cousins. You know how we're always talking about what it is to be Indian/Asian/British etc? So I thought I'd ask real Indians, I mean those born and bred on Bharat's soil, what they think." He switched it on and we sat down on the cushions.

He'd done it really well. The camera spanned over Delhi and my heart did a few flips. I'd only been to India once and that was a rushed, urgent job because of some wedding. But India was the unknown part of me, the unfulfilled, lonely, aching part. That's a major grievance with my parents, so busy making money, they couldn't be bothered to take me to the place that mattered. Mum was very efficient at laying down rules and regulations, but there's not much of the hands-on experience that really meant something.

The titles came up in English and Hindi, flute and sitar music in the background. As we watched he told me about his cousins and family in India. There are lots of funny bits in the film – it followed a group of teenagers around parks, their homes, old buildings and they got tangled up in arguments on whether, as Indians, they should be choosing to do yoga rather than aerobics, and as Indians whether they should think globally and give up fridges and freezers to protect the ozone layer, even though it was the West that had created 'The Hole'. 'How many Indians use hairspray?' asked one, 'or aerosol deodorants?' 'That is a major national problem,' another seemed to agree, elaborately wrinkling up his nose and sniffing loudly, waving his hand as though fending off a hundred nasty odours. They all went for him and he ran for his life, leading them around flower beds, over a bridge, barged into two lovers sharing an ice-cream, bang smack into a picnicking family, who all shook their fists and joined in the chase and so on. By the end he was being chased by a whole posse of people.

It was very funny and I was giggling away. I turned to Suresh and suddenly went silent, we were only inches apart, looking at each other. Caught, encapsulated in feelings that had suddenly become real, hovering between us, waiting for one of us to make a move. Our eyes had gazed and gazed into each other's, then I lowered mine, modestly, waiting... and waiting... and nothing. To hell with that! I opened them and glared at him. What's he up to?

"You have to make the first move," he said.

Me?

"You decide, you set the limits," he insisted.

Me!

I sat up, extremely disgruntled and annoyed. He'd destroyed all the romance. "I can't," I declared. "I haven't been brought up to... to... go around... picking up men," I declared. "I've got inhibitions. And prohibitions." Practically a boast.

He laughed.

Why were people always laughing at me? I flounced away from him.

"You know what those two add up to?" asked Mr Einstein, leaning over towards me. "Inhibition plus Prohibition equals Paralysis! *Samjhi, meri jaan?*" shifting next to me.

That's all I needed, filmi dialogue. How crass can anyone get! (He didn't need to know that even a few words in the Indo-lingo had me melting away with delight). "It's difficult for me. I'm not supposed to," moving away, dropping onto the carpet with a bump.

"Neither am I. Good Indian boy that I am," shifting onto the edge of the cushion, leaning over me, smiling a villainous smile.

"You're half a gorah, Aloo Pakora," suddenly finding a new name for him. My turn to laugh at someone! I escaped to the sofa by the window, not bothering to hide my giggles.

"You try telling my Ma that," coming over,

plonking down next to me, pushing me into a corner. "You know what'll happen to me, if I ever mess up a girl, especially an Indian girl? I'll get boiled in oil," bumping me, squeezing me further into my corner, "roasted in the oven," I was pushing him back, the hog, "and then thrown to the vultures. Alive," and then, we were grappling, fighting for our space, falling off the sofa, all tangled up in a heap... A loud buzzer cut through to us.

"They're coming up here. Quick!" throwing cushions back onto the sofa, quickly feeding another video in. "You sit there, I'm making coffee," he rushed over to his kitchenette and hurriedly started filling up the kettle. There was a knock on the door. It was the Mums, on a tour of the abode. Suresh got very talkative to my Mum, showing her his books, music, videos... a real charmer ain't he!

"Resham, you want to catch up on my family news? Suresh has these videos..." and we spent the next half-hour, cosy and together, sitting in front of the box. Suresh and I were about as comfortable as the cat on the Hot Tin Roof, even though nothing had really happened, had it?

I'm finally given the go-ahead, but not the all-clear. I had to report in, report out, and if it's going to mean being out in the dark, (dark meant the slightest bit of shade) then I must be accompanied by someone, and it could be Suresh, since he seemed like a sensible young man. I nodded eagerly. She looked at me searchingly.

"He's got a girlfriend, Mum."

"So! Do not imagine I do not know anything."

Wouldn't dream of it Mum, I thought to myself. And I could just imagine asking Suresh to look after me and protect me from the dangers of the world.

Weak, frail, female that I am. Except that he was one step ahead of me.

Gazzy and I were in the playground. She was trying to talk to the two yobos. That's what I call them, but Gazzy calls them Robert and Daniel. She thought if she could be friends with them, she'd change them. You can see they were sick with embarrassment, twitching and looking around, silly smiles on their faces. I was enjoying this. Perhaps Gazzy was handling it the right way. By now, I bet they're right sorry they ever made fun of her. Then suddenly Suresh materialised beside us, as if out of nowhere. The yobos seized their chance and vanished from beside us.

"Hi, um, hello." There was an awkward silence. I was feeling nervy, don't know why I should be. I introduced them, but couldn't keep a wobble out of my voice. What must they both have thought? I coughed a little and looked brave, pretending to fight off a dire illness.

Gazzy looked at me puzzled, but started the conversational ball rolling, asking him what he thought about the 'Clean Environment' meeting, since they'd clocked each other there.

They both agreed that the speakers were good. "And I particularly liked the way that Julian Cordell made his points," said Gazzy, "comparing everything to a home. If our homes were as dirty as our towns, we'd refuse to live in them. We don't throw rotting rubbish round in our homes, why should these factories do it in our towns?"

What a pity they hadn't been able to see the video because the TV wasn't working, they both agreed. These two were doing a lot of agreeing, weren't they!

"Sabotage," declared Gazzy, "by the Factory

Polluter's Secret Service." They both laughed.

I was flabbergasted. I didn't know half of what Gazzy's up to these days. She was leading a whole secret life, secret from me anyhow.

"You really threw the councillor..." he was saying to her, looking deep into her eyes.

The man's a male nymphomaniac!

"...when you asked that question about refuse recycling."

Gazzy nodded. Not oblivious to each other's charms, were they! Mr Suresh Kumar Richardson tore his eyes away from Ghazala and tried to focus them in my direction. What a contrast! he must have thought. Oh, I hate him!

"Yesterday was fun, wasn't it?"

There was something quirky going on in his face. What's it about? I nodded, but didn't say anything. Hadn't had time to tell Gazzy about the great reunion yet. She'd misunderstand whatever happens. She didn't know the bet was back on. Haven't had the guts to tell her I'm going ahead with it. But when I looked at him, I just knew I shouldn't. And anyhow what's to say I'd succeed. He liked women like VT Rice. He liked women period! Look at his behaviour with Gazzy.

Yet he was always flaunting his traditional upbringing, I thought sourly. He probably only thought of me as a sister or part of a harem. Doomed either way. All Asian blokes are like that. Double standards! They all practise them. I was working myself up into a real rage. Perhaps I should tell him everything, let him know that he was nothing more than a *thing* and that VT Rice was quite prepared to put him up as the stake in a bet. Except, and my thoughts stopped short, my heart beat went fuzzy, I was the one who started it off, I was the one who suggested it. She's the Good Guy. I'm the Bad Guy. If I cop out, come clean, he'll despise me, I couldn't stomach that. And then my devious mind thought, what if he knew already and he was leading me on? That didn't matter. I'm still the one who started it, I've got to end it. Better to lose now!

"Ma thought you might find this useful," holding out a little tape recorder. "It's much easier to use this than trying to take notes. It works like..."

"I know how these things work." I wanted to keep this short and brutal.

"And it's useful to have a list of questions before you go to an interview. Um have you...do you...want any help?"

"No. Ta."

He looked rather taken aback.

"I've got a list of the people on the committee, and local 'opinion makers' you might want to talk to."

"Jamie's already given it to me."

"Oh," passing his hand through his hair. Oooooh...I did like him doing that, made him look all bothered and bewildered.

"Excellent. You're all organised. I can drive you round to the interviews. Ma's lent me the car."

"No, I don't need to be driven around. Why don't you take VT... Veronica for a spin?" I suggested cattily. She was his girlfriend after all. He'd chosen her, hadn't he? "Perhaps Gazzy would like a lift to your next political meeting."

"Good idea, I was going to do that anyway," turning to go. "I only offered because Ma asked me."

Is this the voice of an angry young man?

"Since you've got everything sorted out, I won't bother you with useless offers of help again.

Goodbye."

"'Bye." I wanted to run after him.

Gazzy looked at me accusingly. Told me I was very rude. I couldn't do anything right for her. I started telling her about VT's deadline. She nodded her head and interrupted, before I had time to finish and tell her why I'd just done what I'd just done. I wanted to complain about the outrageous way he'd been flirting with her.

"Jealousy is wasted energy," was her pious reply. "But Diwali's a good time to wind all this up. We're planning a concert and disco for Diwali."

"Oh, are we?" sidetracking me. "And who's 'we'? And thank you for telling me about it. What's a Muslim doing organising a Hindu festival?"

Gazzy looked at me in disgust and stalked off, then stopped and came back.

"I do what I choose to do. I choose to unite with others. And what makes you think I don't want to have fun? Because of what I wear? Because I pray five times a day? Who's into racist stereotypes now?"

"I'm a beast. Kill me!"

5
THE BEAUTY JUNGLE

Mr Sahani's office was a smart affair in the middle of town, wooden desks, soft chairs and potted plants. His secretary was equally smart, well-cut hair, flawless make-up, crease-free suit. Brought me a coffee and a plate of biscuits, and assured me Mr Sahani would be with me as soon as he's free. Ha! I thought, the dirty old man, Chairman of the Harmony Committee and all he can do is get women to parade on a platform, showing off their bodies, being judged on who's got the best legs and the brightest teeth. Why don't they just get a bunch of horses and give them women's names!

"Miss Somal, how nice to meet you," holding out his hand.

I was too stunned to reply. Here was a Tom Cruise lookalike, an impeccable, trendy dresser, whiffing of subtle aromas of enticement. I felt like a dirty, scruffy schoolgirl.

"Do come through. Did you manage to find the office alright?"

I was ushered into an equally glamorous room, accompanied by expert chit-chat, this wasn't an office...this was a modern boudoir! Paintings on the wall, rugs on the floor, cream-coloured sofas and chairs arranged around a chrome-and-glass coffee table.

"Harjinder, may I call you Harjinder?"

I nodded, unable to trust my voice, as I deliberated

in which armchair to sit.

"What would you like to listen to?" he asked, going over to a CD player.

I gestured vaguely, "Oh, anything is OK." My mind was much too busy trying to work out what's going on. This wasn't his office, why had he brought me here? Everyone was right, wolves were everywhere. What had I got myself into? Had he locked the door?

"Pathana Khan?"

I nodded agreement. Didn't know who he was talking about. Didn't care. I took out the tape-recorder and my notes. "Do you mind if I record the interview?"

"Nope. But why don't you wait 'till Conrad and Varsha are here?"

"Company! I heaved a sigh of relief.

He sat on the sofa. "Surprised at my office huh?"

I nodded again, like a puppet.

"I'm the best at what I do Harjinder, and when you're the best at what you do, you can do what you like." He leaned forward, finger-tapping on the table, eyes bright with enthusiasm. "They, the clients, don't care if you wear torn jeans or Gucci shoes. Or if you don't have a desk in your office. Nothing matters, as long as you come up with the results."

"Call me Hari-jan," I gushed.

"Hari-jan!" he laughed. "You'll definitely have to be the very best to get away with that one. Tell me, Hari-jan, why don't people want to work hard?"

"They do!"

"Then why isn't there more progress? More changes in the world? A better world?"

"People work hard, they get tired, they haven't got time for anything else. They get drained, used up." I'd seen my parents go through every stage of that.

"No, no, no. That's not true," jumping up, hands in pockets, pacing up and down. "Working hard is exhilarating. It actually gives you more energy. We should enjoy our work, do work that's enjoyable and if we're enjoying ourselves, we're happier people. Ipso-facto, we have a happier society."

"Preaching again?" Two people stood in the doorway, both 'professionals' by their appearance, not to mention the briefcases they were carrying. This wasn't my idea of a Harmony Committee! They should be old, dreary, paunchy and boring.

"You promised not to do that," said the man, who must be Conrad. "I do apologise," said he, coming over to shake hands. "He promises not to start lecturing, hectoring, and the minute our backs are turned..."

"I want people to be happier. Don't you want that? Who doesn't want that? I can't understand why people are not happier!" Mukesh spread his arms out, begging the universe for an answer.

"Miss Somal's waiting for an interview, M-u-k-e-s-h-ji," reprimanded Varsha, artificially elongating his name.

"Call me Muck. Doesn't matter, you don't have to be polite in front of her. You should hear the name she's given herself! Muck," whispering to me, "is their name for me. Sweet huh?"

Everybody sat down and calmed down, focusing all their attention on me. Good, I was in charge now, I thought starting off with my first question, beauty contests are degrading to women, because looks shouldn't be something that we get marks and awards for, so why did they choose... I'm not even allowed to finish my question before they all butted in.

"Ours is different... designed to provide opportunities... it's about co-operation... a few mistakes at first... more of a talent contest... on-going training... "

"Quiet!" holding up my hand like a traffic cop. They all fell silent and looked a little shamefaced. "When I get back, I won't be able to make head or tail of what's on this tape. Now one at a time. Varsha, would you like to please tell me why a beauty contest of all things, to promote harmony?"

Giving the others a satisfied smirk, Varsha explained that the idea was to use the normal beauty contest idea to do something different. What they're actually hoping to do was to attract unemployed young women to enter, put them on a three week 'preparation' course. They'd learn about make-up, "...in the sense of a well-groomed appearance," she continued, seeing me about to interrupt, "...clothes, self-presentation in speaking and writing. These are all the skills which you need to land yourself a job."

"Beauty has always been used against women. We're judged on our looks the minute we walk in somewhere, meet someone," I insisted.

"So are men," added Conrad.

"Why do you think I'm so ice-cool, crucial and smart?" Muck straightened his tie and fluttered his eyelashes.

I couldn't help liking him.

"Because women sink or swim because of the way we look. Men are never judged in the same way. Why are you all promoting it, advertising it? Why not one for men?"

Varsha said that if they told me anything more, it's got to be off the record. "Agreed?"

"No," I replied emphatically, "if I can't use it, what's the point of hearing it 'off the record'?"

"It'll help you to understand what we're trying to achieve," said Conrad, leaning forward, hands clasped together, "and perhaps then you won't feel so hostile..."

"I'm not hostile!"

"No?" questioned Muck. "Neither is a rottweiler, I suppose."

Varsha gave him a 'ticking off' look.

"I have an idea, everyone, I've been holed up here since seven-thirty this morning. I have to get out. Hari-jan, where would you like to go? Somewhere where we can all have a drink and snack and talk."

I shrugged my shoulders, I didn't know. I'd never been out (properly, that is) anywhere in this town and I wasn't about to suggest McDonalds to them. Varsha and Conrad tentatively named a few places, both trying to be super-sensitive to my situation as an Asian girl. This was going to turn into a deadlock. "Choose a place," I suggested. "When we get there all I need to do is phone and tell them where I am. But I can't stay long." Relieved smiles from everyone.

The French Bistro it was, with flower bushes in tubs and tables outside. Mentally counting the money in my possession, I declared I wasn't hungry and only wanted a fruit juice.

They all laughed, guessing my predicament.

"You're a journalist, aren't you? Put it on expenses!" Conrad teased.

Varsha organised them, told Muck to order something for us and hustled me off to the phone. "I've got to phone my husband too."

"And I've got to go and fix my face," pouted Conrad, following us around the side of the building.

Mum and Dad were busy so I quickly gave the details and got back to the table first.

"I've ordered you every fruit juice on the menu," announced Muck. He started telling me funny stories about his clients.

"Americans are the worst and the best to work with but you do wonder how some of them got where they have. For instance, Buckleigh Masters. American. First time he came to see me, he ate up everything put in front of him. We got more food, he ate that up, more food, he ate that up. Teresa, my assistant, was going crazy trying to keep up the supply. After an hour, a whole hour, he belched, loud and long, like this..." daring me to stop him.

I dared him to do it.

"Cultural confusions, that's what it was all about. I was thinking, American greed. He was thinking, Oriental hospitality, must not insult. In this day-and-age too! You'd think their education system would have brought itself up-to-date, with the way the Japanese are buying up America. Nothing doing. They just hide deeper in their old racist habits. That's enough shop talk. Now," leaning forward confidentially, "tell me about yourself."

I just had to laugh. He was so OTT.

"What's a journalist like you doing on a story like this?" leaning even further forward, trying to tangle eyelashes.

"You trying to count the spots on my face? You go back to your own fruit juice, Mr Muck." Then I felt myself being watched, you know how sometimes you get this prickly feeling. I looked up, straight into Suresh's eyes. I half-lifted my hand to say 'Hi', but there was nothing friendly in those eyes. He turned away and left, joining an elderly man who'd

obviously been waiting for him. I made an effort to
get back into the bantering tone, but I was empty
inside, I had lost something. I did my best to smile
and chat when the others came back. I took some
notes about their 'project', as they called it, but my
mind was feeble. Promised to think about it and get
back in touch with them, wanting to make a quick
escape. Of course Varsha couldn't just let me go and
catch a bus, I had to wait and then let her drive me
home. I told her I was unconvinced. "Seems to me,
you're a bunch of well-off yuppies with nothing to
do except think up harebrained schemes."

She assured me they had lots to do but they
wanted to do more. I was invited to her office to talk
out the nitty-gritties of it.

6
SINGIN' THE BLUES

Everything's a blur, all action is mechanical. I tried not to think. Did my chores in the house, all my homework was on time, and I'd been nice to everyone. I didn't notice the puzzled looks that followed me around. I played my tapes, watched TV. Everything was elastoplast, nothing healed. I didn't expect this kind of pain. I couldn't understand it. It's not as though we actually got together. And what right did he have to look at me the way he did? He always had VT. He never said anything about that. He was going to hang on to her 'till he was sure of me, was he? Just because he saw me talking to someone he goes jumping to conclusions as high as Everest! Men! Always double standards! I really tried to work myself up into a lather, hoping to get so angry, all the pain would evaporate. Didn't work. Seeing him turn his back, just done me in.

"...*udaas raat hai... zuban pe dard...*" passing Mum and Dad's room late at night, midnight mug of cocoa clutched in my hands, a song seeping under the door, rooted me to the spot. "...*Udaas raat hai...*" Words, the voice, flowed around me, music that melted through my skin.

A strange sensation of recognition, that went beyond the walking-talking 'Everyday Me', homed into and connected with something inside, another 'Me'?

Another 'Me' who'd lain ignored, suppressed and was now awakening, as though my unhappiness and pain had given it permission to come out. As though I needed more for myself, from myself, than the 'Workaday Me', geared to survival in school and street, could provide. I'd pushed deep away somewhere all the parts that didn't synchronise with the 'English Corporate Image'. And if you pushed parts of yourselves away, they left empty spaces behind.

I realised now that Mum had tried to rescue some of that, keep it going with her rules and regulations. But that's all they had been to me, rules and regulations imposed on me, not something I wanted from inside of me.

This other 'Me' took life from the familiarity of sounds, images, thoughts that came from its part of my self.

Dazed I slipped down, to nestle on the floor. The song, its sounds, its Udaasi, dissolved the line between me and the night. No separation between what I felt and what existed outside, no separation between me and the world around me. A homecoming.

In the morning, opening the curtains, it all felt like a dream. Was there really another 'Me'? Another 'Me' that had lain trapped, in exile?

"Rubbish," I declared, and immediately felt bad, like a villain killing off a fairy. I'd never killed off a fairy after I'd read what Tinkerbell said in *Peter Pan*. Not that I'd ever have admitted this to anyone else. There are some things that one keeps to oneself. "I take that back," I said to the other 'Me'. I wrote out 'sorry' on my skin, promising not to forget, promising to look after this other 'Me'. Last night everything had seemed so clear, this morning it was rather cloudy and confused.

Language can't make all that much difference, can it? Language is for communication, and I communicated quite well, thank you.

"No wonder you're emotionally handicapped!" retorted the other 'Me'.

Hardly a day old and it was already getting aggressive with me. Emotions and language? This stuff was too heavy for me, man. I'm going back to dozyland right now. 'Bye, 'bye.

"What about last night then, eh? That song had you drooling through your teardrops, didn't it?"

It was as stubborn as me, this other 'Me'.

"Before, they were just in black-and-white, (pun fully intended). And now they're fully grown, no gaps, no half parts..."

"And bloody painful too."

"Good morning, Harjinder."

Oh hell, it was Mum!

"Talking to the spirits?" She was carrying a cup of tea, and holding it out to me. She'd never done that before. Something had definitely happened to the world. It must have shifted on its axis. No wonder I was feeling the way I was. Did the sun rise in the West today? I must get the papers and read all about it.

"Yes," said my mother patiently.

My head jerked up.

"This tea is for you. Would you like me to hold it for you while you drink it?"

The next day, I dug out my Walkman, raided Mum's music collection and shoved half-a-dozen tapes into my bag, before rushing off to school... And amongst them all, I discovered the perfect tape, *Talat in a Blue Mood*. It's great, it's sad, it made me want to cry and cry. And then it made me want to kick my head in, for wasting all this precious emotion on that hot-tempered, double-standard, harami, stupid idiot.

It's not as though anything actually happened between us. 'Waiting for me to make the first move' he'd said so coyly. Well, I would! I wasn't going to weep and wail, waiting for him to come to his senses.

I picked up the phone, resolute and determined. Dialled his number, got his Imperial Majesty on the phone. Kicked the frog out of my voice, started off with the normal courtesies and what did I receive in return? Freezing tones, that chilled me to me bones.

Bravely, I persisted and in an off-hand way, mentioned the French Bistro, thinking I'm opening the door to sort it out.

Mr Thundercloud informed me he was just on his way out and since he'd already been delayed, he'd be terribly late. Goodbye!

He's hung up on me! I'm left staring at the receiver. I didn't deserve this. How could he! He's a monster. Hate is what he deserved but all I'd got are tears.

I went to see my Masi. I didn't mean to tell her anything. But when she put her arms around me, muttering soothing, comforting sounds, smoothing my hair as though I was a child, I blurted it all out.

I suppose I was hoping for that sagacious, sort-out-your-troubles kind of advice, that pithy wisdom that elders deliver in a sentence so readily to the young in books and films. Masi carried on holding me, mopping up my tears, uttering those no-word sounds that were all sympathy and love.

"You know, Baby, the hardest thing about growing old is seeing your children unhappy. Seeing them suffer and not being able to do anything about it. If we could, we'd all do Jantramantra and make it alright."

"But if everyone could do Jantramantra it still wouldn't help Masiji, because everyone would keep changing things round to the way they want them. There'd be even more emotional chaos."

"Shabash. Ma jini akal hai. But remember one thing, your magic is that you are loved. You are worth loving. You haven't done anything wrong. Love yourself, Beti. Let that ...boy come to his senses."

I can't repeat what she said, I'll get done under the Obscenities Act.

I kicked the counter as I sat down to do my evening duty at the till. You ever tried holding together a broken heart, listening to lines like *Chal Akela* etc and ringing up four pounds, twenty-five, coffee jar, seventy-nine pence, sweets, one pound ten for four pints of milk. Then being handed a ten pound note, and then giving the ten pounds back in change.

"Er, love," knocking on my Walkman, I don't switch it off. "You know what you done..." speaking loudly and pointing to the money.

I raised my eyes ceilingwards. It needed painting, perhaps we could get an artist to do it: *'The Sistine Supermarket!'*

"You've gone and..."

Yes I know, I wanted to say, take it and go. Run!

"Here you are love. We all make mistakes."

I waggled my head and 'thankyouthankyou'd' her 'till she was out the door. Honestly! Why couldn't she just keep it? I wouldn't have minded an argy-bargy when the till didn't add up.

I cornered Mum in her office and asked where I could learn Hindi.

Reluctantly removing her gaze from her computer module, she examined me with her X-ray eyes.

"Do not wear the Walkman day-and-night, Harjinder, it will ruin your ears. About its effect on the brain I will keep silent, for I do not have much hope in that department. When you have finished with my tapes, Harjinder, please make sure you put them back exactly where you got them from. Some of them are classics, and many of them impossible to buy now."

"Hindi, Mummyji! I asked you about Hindi."

"Why?"

"Pardon?"

"Why this sudden enthusiasm for Hindi?"

She had me on the Hot Spot and it was most uncomfortable. So I can understand these songs better and be even more unhappy? Instead I waffled, and she didn't listen with patience.

"Last time we found you a class you would not go."

"Yuck, yuck," I feigned a vomit into the rubbish bin. "The teacher, all the kids called him Yuck Yuck."

The phone gave a genteel ring. You know by now, how genteel me Mum is.

"I will think about it, now go away," such motherly love.

I ripped open a box of canned peas when someone tapped me on the shoulder.

Mum called, "Telephone for yoo-ooh!"

My heart did twenty somersaults in a second, though there's no reason why. I ran off to answer it.

It's Binny. My cousin who's in love with the Marks and Spencer's *Kwality Man*. She was bubbling over with happiness, I had to hold the receiver five inches away from my ear, the avalanche of excitement could do permanent damage.

"Introduction meeting is on Sunday, this coming Sunday!"

I could hear her jumping up and down.

"Come with Uncle and Aunty. I'm taking time off work, I've booked everything, facial, make-up, hair - the lot. But 'Jindi, I can't decide whether to wear a sari, or shalwar kameez. Are churidaars out or in? I saw some in a boutique, but then someone said they're out. And what do you think of lungi-style shalwar, is that too high fashion? I don't want to look old-fashioned, but I mustn't be too... too... fashionable, if you see what I mean... And should it be chappels, sandles or shoes. After all, it's at home...I saw a gorgeous yellow sari, but I wondered whether that might be too dramatic..." Binny talked, I listened.

I could see Mummy pointing to the clock. Fifteen minutes already.

"Binny, Binny," managing to interrupt, "got to go, slave time here, I saw Masi yesterday, why didn't she tell me?" Nobody told me anything, they either walked away or hung up on me.

"Because it hadn't been confirmed, you idiot. How could she tell you if she didn't know. Do you think I should try to get something at that new boutique, *Lajwaab* ? It's just that it's so far and I'll have to take another day off work, and half their gear looks like it should be worn at a coronation. Now, I've got a suit made from one of Mum's old saris..."

Mum tapped my shoulder, made a chopping

motion with her hands, I'm not sure whether it was meant for me or the phone.

"Binny, listen. I've got it, the pale blue silk, shot through with hints of amber, delicately embroidered in silver, frock-style shalwar kameez, teamed with plain chiffon dupatta, court shoes, pearl earings, simple silver bracelet sounds good... *Oh Gawd*, have I just ruined her life?

"How's the video man?"

"Who?"

"Who, You-Know-Who. Bhindi-Fingers."

Mum could hear every word, even whilst busy in her business. I tried to wrap up the call and told her I'll see her Sunday.

"'Jindi, seems to me you give up too easy. You gotta fight for what you want."

I plonked down the receiver. It was too late for any kind of kind advice.

The following evening was my appointment with Varsha. Non-stop action woman aren't I! Our arguments went backwards and forwards and I was quite aggressive 'cos I was just feeling sore at the whole world. Eventually she pulled out the files on their 'project', showing me the outline of the preparation courses. They're very detailed with aims and objectives clearly stated, course content worked out and divided into different stages.

"You'll get the dregs and the racists."

Gazzy should be in with this lot.

"That's the experiment. And don't let me hear you say that again."

"'Be nice to everyone week', is it? Love and care will change the world."

Using up many a tissue, and listening to Asif Ghazali's luscious voice on Radio Asia, I finished the first article on the Beauty Contest and dropped it into Mr God Almighty's cubbyhole, with a note to explain it was part of a series, so there'd be more to follow.

Searching high and low for Gazzy. Up the stairs, down the stairs, I even landed up in the school basement.

"Oi you! Get out of it," Mr Driscoll-Clean-Sweep-Caretaker, put down a body-builder's bells.

"Just looking for a friend," meekly backing towards the stairs.

"Oh yeah, I know all about these friends. Wouldn't happen to be a friend of the opposite sex, would it?"

He was big and muscly.

"You kids! Think you can get away with your lies and fornication. I'm going to have trip wires set up here in this basement, I am. All you kids think you can slip in 'ere for your bit of *canoodle-cadoodle*. And it don't stop there, I'm disgusted to say."

He was at the bottom of the stairs, blocking my way.

"You should see the things I find in 'ere. Regular devil's den. You kids can't do it at home, so you reckon you can carry on your trickery in this 'ere basement. Well I'm not having it. Neither's my friend Mr Rizvi from the Mosque, or my friend Mr Purewal from the Gurudwara, or my friend Mr Bahl from the Mandir. Get it? You kids been let run wild too long. What's your name girl?" taking out a notebook and pen.

"Why?"

"Don't ask me why!" Roaring, the sound echoing from floor to roof. "We're keeping tabs on you, our moral crusade is on the march. Now. Name!"

"Oh, sure, uh, Siridevi. That's... um... let me spell it

for you. S-i-r-i first name and D-e-v-i surname. I'm going to be late for class, can I go now please?"

"All right, but you just watch out, Old Driscoll's right 'ere, keeping his eyes on you," voice following me as I scampered up the stairs. "Hey, isn't there an actress...?"

I was out. Phew phew phew!

Wow, I didn't know 'things' went on in the basement! Here I was thinking I'm a real smart-aleck know-all and I didn't know the half of it.

Better finish an essay before the angel of vengeance came tapping on my shoulder. In the study area, I walked bang smack into Gazzy and her gang (the ones that I call 'the yobos' and she calls Richard and Daniel). She was helping them with their maths.

"Look Gaz, as far as these two are concerned, two plus two equals wogs out."

"Look Hari, go away." Then she called me back. "On till duty tonight?"

I shook my head mournfully, like I was really sad.

"OK, then come to the Diwali Planning Meeting, room eight. Oh, by the way, Suresh was looking for you."

Was he? Why? Couldn't be anything important. I'd ignore it, I won't go chasing after him. Or should I? I couldn't go to him, I couldn't trust myself to behave normal. Perhaps he wanted to apologise and explain. That'd be nice to hear. And in turn, I could get a few things off my chest. Go the whole hog, tell him about the bet too and how my head's been going around in circles, deadlocked with suspicions and suppositions.

Five minutes before Eng Lit class, I dashed off to the *Spanner* office. Taking a deep breath, and gathering up my courage, I knocked on the door. No answer. Again, loudly. Jamie opened the door abruptly, his tousled appearance immediately gave him away despite the quick smile he flashed on. You can just whiff it out, can't you? You don't even need to see the other person, hiding out of sight. Here's one couple that didn't need to creep into the dangerous privacy of the basement.

By the end of the day I was just exhausted, it was like my insides had been churned around in a cement mixer. If Gazzy hadn't been there to drag me along to her Diwali Committee I would have headed straight for the bus and home.

Gazzy's multi-cultural pack. It had her stamp all over it. About a dozen kids, a mix of girls and boys – Asians, Greeks, Afro-Caribbean, English, Jewish – the lot. Her mini-United Nations. I nearly turned back at the door, "This lot, is going to plan Diwali?" I hissed incredulously.

"Hari, if you go away I'll never speak to you again," she hissed back at me. "I need you. This is my idea. It's got to work."

Her hold on my arm had turned into a vice.

"After Diwali, we'll do Christmas, Eid etc, with the same bunch. You get the idea?"

I got the idea. I was resigned. What price friendship? Heavy, I can tell you.

"Would you like to release my arm, before it shrivels up from lack of blood?"

I sat down at a table, the rest were chatting and laughing. I drew doodles on my pad. Half the time would be spent on explanations about Diwali, some won't hear a word, others will misunderstand. We'll go through it all over again and again...

"Hello."

I looked up. Oh hell, it was him! I looked around

for VT, she couldn't be far behind.

"Can I talk to you for a moment? Outside."

I just nodded and followed dumbly. He stopped at a little archway half-way down the corridor.

"Have a nice evening at the Bistro?"

"I rang you to explain."

"You needn't have worried. I don't snitch."

"That's nonsense."

"I understand why you didn't want me along. You could've just told me. Or don't you believe in telling the truth? After I met you in the video shop you joked about lying - the joke was on me, in believing you! What really makes me mad is the goody-goody Indian girl, ghee-wouldn't-melt-in-my-mouth bit, getting everybody running round in circles making elaborate arrangements for you."

"I'd never met Mukesh before that evening, you stupid cretin!"

"Fast work! You girls are always accusing us of double standards, but you really did a number on me. I thought I was being thoughtful, not wanting to rush you or pressurise you. Wimp! that's my label..."

"You haven't been honest with me..." managing to force my way into the 'conversation'.

"First time you meet him, it just happens to be a dinner date, you're kissing the bloke in public..."

"Stop it, how dare you! I wasn't. You're so jealous, you won't listen to the truth."

"I'm not jealous. I don't care. But when two people have their heads together like you did, they're discussing the weather, are they? If you need more excuses to meet him, I'm not going to be your front..."

"You never were. And there were two other people there, you blind bat..."

"Your invisible friends? I'm not falling for that and I'm not falling for this rigmarole about doing a whole series of articles on the Beauty Contest or this whitewash of an article!" waving my pages at me. "You're supporting the Beauty Contest! When I asked you to do this, I thought I'd get something intelligent from you..."

"I'm not letting you get away with this, you're behaving just like every other hot tempered, self-centred bloke that's ever lived. You've been boasting about your traditional upbringing, well it certainly shows...you see me with a man, for half a second, jump to your own conclusions, and then refuse to listen to an explanation."

"You didn't want me along. You made that clear."

"Because I don't need to be 'babbied' and because..." I took a deep breath, here goes...

"Fine. I understand that. I won't bother you with expressions of care and concern again, but I only take work that's interesting and intelligent. This doesn't make the grade, in fact you've never made the grade..."

"That's vicious." And to think I had scruples about the bet!

"Sorry if this makes it inconvenient for you to arrange your assignations. This episode, your journalistic adventure, as far as I'm concerned, is over."

"How dare you!" When I thought of the amount of work I'd put into this one, and into planning the others, I could've whacked him.

"I knew it. You never intended to publish. You never accept any of my work. You've been leading me on, stringing me along. You've had things your way for far too long. You think you're God and you act like you're God. Well I'm gonna get you. I'm going to be Editor next year, I'll break your stranglehold. I'll put some life and excitement into that stuffy rag, and furthermore, thank you for not publishing my articles, because I'm going to publish in the newspapers."

"You're always threatening to go elsewhere. Good luck!"

"And what about VT...Veronica?" I was so angry I wanted to slice him up.

"What about her?"

"You've had a girlfriend all this time that I...that we..." I gave up trying to find the right words. "Goodbye!" I marched off, then marched back and held out my hand. "Since you don't want it, I'll have my work back."

"No. I'd like to keep it."

"You want to keep it and stick pins in it?" My hands were clenched into fists. Me staring at him, him staring at me.

"Do you two know," Gazzy inquired, "that you can be heard by everyone?"

"Race you back, Gaz," taking her arm and trotting her off. "Can't wait to get stuck into your Diwali plans."

I volunteered as Secretary. What with my schoolwork, my journalism, my contribution to the family economy and now this Diwali business, I won't have a second to think of anything else.

And I must say, I was very surprised by the knowledge and contributions of all present. They'd all been reading up on Diwali, apparently Gazzy had insisted on that as part of the condition for being on the Committee.

There was a debate on whether to have it

traditional or modern. Should there be a full puja ceremony or just a concert and disco and a good time to be had by all?

"We have to have divas, perhaps on the stage or all around the window ledges," said Sharon

"Fire hazard. Won't be allowed." It was Mr God Almighty. When did he sidle in? "Fairy lights, everyone uses them."

"How artificial!" I was critical.

Someone suggested a theme Diwali, for instance it could be the Mahabharat.

"That's a great idea. But wrong book, wrong period," Okon waving his finger admonishingly. "The Ramayan it is and the Ramayan it has to be. The spectacle, the glamour, the thrills and spills – Ram, Sita, and their furry furred friend Hanuman-Monkeyman, battle against that big bad baddy Ravan."

He got some applause.

"No, no, no," Chanchal groaned and shook his head vehemently. "No way! It'll look like those horrible tacky Diwali plays we had to do in Junior School. I say we keep it simple, get a top Bhangra band and boogie all night."

"And charge the earth!"

"Nothing as cheap as that. This things got to have class."

"A lot of the girls won't be able to come."

"Girls? No problem. I can provide coachloads."

All hell broke loose. Not quite but nearly. Chanchal loved every minute of it.

Gazzy brought out a little hammer and rapped it loudly, three times. Now I know what she's going to do when she grows up!

"*Ardour! Ardour!*" shouted someone mimicking an

old Indian song, and everyone went silent, busily trying to work out if they should be thinking of sex or business.

"We seem to be at a deadlock," Gazzy calmly ignored the heckling... 'Miss IQ two hundred here'... 'fantastic summary'. "Since some of us have responsibilities back home..."

"Join the anti-antidisestablishmentarians and annihilate your bondage." Tom Thumb, who endeavoured to compensate for his lack of inches by cultivating verbal giant*ism*.

The hammer rapped again, everyone cowered in fear. Gazzy's stern voice held us in its vice, "We're not talking about Diwali ten years from now. Right, this is the game plan. Write your suggestions on a piece of paper, you got ten minutes. Give them to Hari, they'll be printed out by the next meeting, when we'll decide which one to go for by democratic vote."

"What if we want half of one plan, quarter of another and a percentage of a third?" asked maths-mad Ivana.

"We'll be here 'till doomsday!"

Almighty God politely put up his hand to be heard. All went silent in anticipation. What's this power he's got? He suggested a sub-committee of five to collate the ideas and come up with the three best plans. Approved by an overwhelming majority. I wrote that down.

Everyone volunteered to be on the sub-committee.

Gazzy groaned, then took it upon herself to choose.

"Oh no, not me," I protested meekly, as her jabbing finger came round to me.

"Secretary has to," said Mr Know-All who didn't know a thing.

I resign, I was about to say. And then thought, why give him the satisfaction? Anyhow, I might need the work experience.

"What was all that shouting about?" asked Gazzy, as she kept me company at the bus stop. "Sounded like a lovers' quarrel."

I frowned and looked at her very sternly. What she doin' sayin' things like that?

"How's the bet?"

Give over Gaz, I wanted to say.

"Once a gambling woman, always a gambling woman." I kicked the bus-stop post. I could've kicked the whole world. Not doing my Reeboks any favours. They're in a fine state of deterioration. I stared at them sadly.

7

WHAT THE PAPERS SAY

I posted my work of genius to the local rag and during the next week lived in dread and apprehension. If they rejected it, then he – Thingy – would surely find out. The final humiliation! My mother had taken to hovering around me. Opening her mouth to say something, then shutting it again. Sitting next to me on the sofa when I'd try to drown my sorrows in TV soaps. Squeezing my arm as a sign of motherly affection. I'd pointed out the bruises to her.

The newspaper phoned and said they're interested but it needed editing and would I go and see them. Would I! I went to see Muck and the others and they were all dead delighted. Not many contestants had come forward and a newspaper article might just ignite those fires of ambition.

"You didn't make our underlying plan too obvious?" asked Varsha worriedly. "It'll just frighten off women who have a low confidence threshold."

How about my confidence threshold? I wanted to say. It's below zero these days. Muck gave me a piece of paper and asked if I knew anything about it. The top line had skull bones and crosses and the bottom was a line of fire flames. In between was a badly spelt warning against 'poofter do-gooders'.

"Looks like someone needs to go to art school!" I said, but promised to keep my ears open and see what I could find out. I could just imagine it was those silly boys who've seen too many gangster movies. I'd give it to Gazzy to handle, I decided, she could get her two yobos to find out more.

My threshold heated up to an equatorial high when I came out in black-and-white, courtesy of *Mercury*, 'your indispensable organ of news, views and information'. Their slogan, not mine.

I didn't know so many people read the papers. Even those types you would have thought had better uses for newsprint. Gazzy's yobos, her Richard and her Daniel, came over and asked if it was really me who wrote it all.

"Did you get someone to read it to you?" I asked sweetly.

"We just wanted to warn you 'cos you're Ghazala's friend."

Fancy them being able to say her name, so proper like!

"There might be trouble comin' up and you could be in it."

I raised my very practiced brow.

"We'll find out what we can about the other thing. But no more meetings. We'll deal through Ghazala."

Pure *Miami Vice*. I can feel the heat.

"Congratulations!" It was VT Rice. "Who's a big celebrity star, hey? The school mag not good enough for you? Or was it the other way round?"

She looked at me with those big mascarad eyes, pretending innocence, waiting for an answer. I stayed silent. I wasn't rising to the bait. As though she didn't know.

Fingers fumbled on my back. I was being mugged in the middle of the school corridor! I swung round and it was two big cretins from the Sixth Form trying to pin something on me. They were giggling and laughing and we chased each other like a dog chasing its tail. It was VT who reached through the silly circling and snatched the paper from them. It was a copy of my article with a headline of their own – 'Scoop! Scoop! Confessions of a Schoolgirl!' VT looked disgusted and tore it up. Taking my arm, she moved me away from them.

"Penalties of fame. There are those who hate those who succeed."

"Congratulations!"

It wasn't VT repeating herself. It was Mr You-Know-Who, who thought he ruled the universe, repeating VT. He was behind me in the queue for the nosh. I hadn't noticed him before. Bet he pushed in. I ignored him. I ordered my cauliflower cheese, chips and samosas, ladled a lake of custard onto my apple crumble, and in high dungeon, walked off to a table. There was a spare chair, which I pointedly moved away. He came and placed his tray in front of mine and pointedly brought back the chair.

"How does it feel to be published?" he asked, and added "at last."

I put my fork down. I'd suffered enough. "Look, I come in here because I need to eat. I don't come in here because I need aggro. You chose to come and sit at my table. I didn't invite you. Therefore, the least you can do is be polite. If you can't be polite, then be quiet. And if you can't be quiet, then please move away!"

"That wasn't very nice of me. I'm sorry."

Mr Master of the Universe apologising to insignificant little me? My day was made. Nothing could top this one.

"I have a message for you. Ma asked if you would like to come to tea."

Well well! This was the one that couldn't be

topped. Pukka sure. *Mummy ne apko chai ke liya bulaiya* came singing into my mind, you don't need a mind when the Hindi movies have gone and done it for you already. I looked at him and the hint of a smile in his eyes said he heard it too.

"Well, I don't think so." I was reluctant. Just like the hero on the receiving end of that song. "I would have to discuss it with my Mum."

"That's been done. Ma spoke to her this morning. She's quite happy about it."

Thank you! I said to my Mum, but no thank you. Arranging marriages was one thing, that's history and tradition, you're allowed to do it. Arranging tea parties for me without my agreement was modern and permissive, that, you're not allowed to do.

"Why?" I asked his regular question.

"Beg pardon?" He sat right in front of me, he'd asked a question, then calmly forgotten all about it in the passing of half a second and wandered off to think of something else, probably someone else.

"Forgotten what you asked me?" He was making me really irritable. I was in serious danger of not enjoying my apple crumble.

"No, not at all. Will you be able to come?"

His strange jigsaw face was quite fascinating, it kept moving, changing, becoming something new...No! I wasn't going to go.

"Ma was very impressed by your article."

"Well, she's an intelligent woman. Unlike her son." It was meant to hurt and be deeply wounding. I watched carefully but could detect no reaction. He must have been working on the inscrutable face. "Please tell Aunty Laxmi that I shall phone her." Boy! Was I on top form today or was I not? What a supremely clever way of giving him his come-uppance and saying yes! I almost felt sorry for him as I got up and piled the dishes on my tray.

He asked if I was going off to class now and I gave him my best supercilious look. What did he think I came to school for?

"Will you be popping into the ladies', before you go to class?"

Well really! Hands on my hips. I was back into high dungeon. What would any girl think of a question like that?

"If you're not," he said sweetly, getting up with the tray in hand, "I should wipe that big blob of custard off your nose now. Goodbye." He smiled as he turned and walked away from me, even his back was smiling.

Binny called, brimming over with excitement as usual. Happiness is not infectious, I was living proof. At the interview/introduction meeting, the families had agreed that the two young people should have time to meet before any big decisions were taken.

"He invited me to lunch at that really smart new place..."

She talked so fast, my brain had to race to keep up with her.

"...The French Bistro." I closed my eyes. Terrible things happened there, I wanted to say, it was cursed.

"It was brilliant! Conversation was a bit slow at first, you know how it is, both of us a little nervous and then you came to the rescue, broke the ice!"

I did? I bolted upright. How? When I was miles and miles away...

"Ash said..."

"Ash?" I queried quick as a flash, managing to interrupt.

"Ashok, but everyone calls him Ash and he said I should too."

Is that a blush I hear?

"Ash said had I seen this very interesting article in the paper by someone called Harjinder and then I said, well actually, she's my cousin and I told him lots about you and how your parents have helped us since Dad died. And then he talked about his family and what it was like when they lived in Kenya and about his brother and sister. He's the eldest..."

I made myself comfortable and settled down to listen. Half-an-hour later, she decided it's time to go and pluck her eyebrows, re-do her nails and get her clothes ready for the next day.

"Wait!" I yelled, just as she was about to hang up. "What happens next?"

"Oh, that. I talk to my Mum. He talks to his Mum. They talk to the vicholi, you know, the go-between..."

"I know what it means!" I shouted into the phone. Why did everyone think I didn't know anything?

Binny went into a huff. "'Jindi, you're in such a temper these days, it's impossible to talk to you. And you haven't visited us for ages. Come round soon. Goodnight!"

I was left staring at the phone. I put it back. It rang. Binny calling to really grovel this time. I picked it up and didn't answer. Neither did the person at the other end. A heavy breather! I'd never had a nasty call before. I shall be very, very rude.

"Hello. May I speak to Harjinder, please?"

"Gazzy!"

"Ouch! Now listen, don't interrupt, my money will run out soon. Hari-jan, just shut up and listen. I want to talk to you. Come to school early. You only have to get yourself out of bed half-an-hour earlier. Don't moan. I'll meet you at your bus-stop. Goodnight."

I was left staring at the phone. Again.

8
CLOSED CIRCUIT

Having faithfully followed orders and sacrificed half-an-hour of sleep, I jumped off the bus all agog to meet Gazzy. She wasn't there. Typical! I was about to think, except it wasn't. The new Gazzy was not only a new leaf turned over, she's a born-again goody gum drops. So this was more than unusual.

I leaned against a shop window, watching 'life's parade' passing by:

'What is this life, if full of care,
We have no time to stand and stare.'

Right on brother! This was my quality time, to stand and stare. When I can, that is, in-between picking up suspicious looks, getting pushed, jostled and being moved on by the shopkeeper who was putting out his boxes of vegetables. They took up half the pavement and no-one pushed them around. Even they have a place in this world, I thought jealously. Me? I'm a *wog*, a *female*. An unwanted *Brit-Cit*. An unwanted *daughter*. Mum and Dad had never let on, that after two daughters they would have quite liked a little male piddling round the house. It's my Dadima, my Dad's mother, who'd heave huge sighs when she saw me and said, in a roundabout, fully-meaning-to way that it's such a pity my grandfather's name will die out.

I examined the dirty gutter and was about to ask myself those great questions of life, you know like: What am I doing here? In this world? On this earth?

"Hey!" A sharp stab of pain as something hit my ankles. It was the wheels of a double buggy being pushed by a poor harassed woman, who obviously didn't even have time to drag a comb through her hair. She desperately muttered apologies to me, trying to referee between her fighting kids while manoeuvring the awkward contraption, around obstacles and the on-coming human traffic. Perhaps there's an answer for me somewhere there.

Double Jeopardy! The film title stared out at me from the video shop. Sums it all up, don't it?

I looked at my watch. At this rate, I was actually going to end up being late for school. If I'd known she was going to take this long I could have sat in McDonalds, forcing myself to drink their coffee. Instead of thinking complicated thoughts about existence, I could have been getting on with living. Drinking coffee and liking it was the next item on my agenda of skills. (I've mastered the eyebrow trick, me and my mirror are well pleased). If you wannabee a *wannabee*, you had to drink coffee like you just loved it to death.

Madam dashed up just as I'd given up on her. She was out of breath, cheeks flushed and trying to talk in-between gasps. There's nothing for it, I took her arm and steered her towards the Big M. I got her a cup of water, a cup of juice and a cup of tea. I waited patiently. I was the personification of patience.

"Had to talk to someone, thought of you," taking sips from all the cups.

She'd be sick. I moved the tea and juice away from her, and told her to drink one at a time.

"My aunt arrived from Bradford. With my cousin. A week ago actually. She knows what a weird family our's is. But she...she's...she..." grabbed the juice and

107

downs it in a gulp, "...she's suggested to my Mum about marriage between me and my cousin."

I raised my eyes heavenwards and shook my head. Why didn't I guess? Everyone around me was marriage mad, and here I was, single, solitary and sad.

"You don't have to, Gaz. No-one in the world can force you. I'm on your side and I'll fight for you to the end!"

She picked up the glass of water but her trembling hand splashed it all over the table.

"Hari. That's not the problem," leaning towards me, whispering. "I think I want to."

I want that coffee, I thought. I went to get it and then I told her we had five minutes before we had to race off.

"Gaz. You got exams coming up." I have to talk her out of this madness! "You want to be a doctor. You said so. You got the brains for it, not many of us can say that. You got respect. Not one of us got that. The school, the elders, even the yobos, everyone respects you. You're a sickening model of perfection. You can do what you want! Why do you want to do this?"

She drew patterns in the spilt water, she looked out of the window, she looked completely confused. This wasn't my Gazzy. I pointed to my watch and held up three fingers. Time waits for no woman.

"I...um...they're very rich, they own a string of restaurants, and my aunt, she really loves Amma. It's her way of helping out. If I was married off so well, then Mum and Dad wouldn't have to worry, and their lives would be much easier." Gazzy stopped.

I'm shocked out of my skin.

"You'd marry for money?" I couldn't even whisper, it was a hiss.

"You think I should marry for love?" she hissed back.

I couldn't answer her, it wasn't just one way or the other, 'cos you can see the being in love business doesn't work out that great either.

"Marrying for money is obscene!"

We're like two boxers in a ring, leaning towards each other, heads almost touching, hissing and spitting.

"Marrying for love is obscene too! It don't stop women getting beaten up, it don't stop divorce, it don't stop the kids getting torn apart. I see it every day where I live. I don't like love. That's fact. My problem is," her voice falling to below whisper level, and trailing off, "knowing all this, seeing all this, I've gone and fallen for it too. I think I've fallen in love!"

I smiled. Aha, she was normal after all!

"But I don't trust that. Do you think I should?"

I shook my head, meaning 'No', meaning 'I don't know', meaning 'I'm confused too'.

"And anyhow, I'd decided not to get married. And I don't like changing my mind. But, Hari, I...I have feelings, desires. I mean, I just want to be near him all the time. It's terrible, I'm out of control."

"Rather quick, isn't it? All this true love and passion erupting in a week."

"I've seen him all my life, off and on, you know, on visits and so forth. We've sort of grown up together, and I've...always thought that he was rather interesting."

"Fancied him, did you? Never said a word about it to me. Honestly Gaz! I don't know why I put up with you."

"Shut up, Hari. I've got to give an answer by the weekend. What do I do?"

"Run. Time's up!"

Gazzy got in everywhere. Busy trying to do my work, she was tramping round my brain, trying to sort out her problem. Honestly! I thought, shaking my head. She was the last person to get into a pickle like this. She was the one who gave cut and dried answers to all *my* confusions, she's the one who gives *me* a ticking off for going off the rails...

"I see, Harjinder. You're shaking your head, you don't agree with the idea of fate in Thomas Hardy's novels..." Mr Martin, looking inquiringly over his glasses at me.

He was too young to be doing that, it was all part of his calculated style.

"You believe that we have free will and everything that happens is our responsibility?"

"I think it's a bit of everything, sir."

"That's a very nice way of sitting on the fence." He perched himself on an empty desk in front of us.

He was always well-dressed, hair slicked back. A dead-ringer for Jordan, you know, New Kids on the Block. Half the girls in school felt obliged to fancy him.

"I'm not sitting on the fence sir! We're born into a world that's already got set ideas on what white people do, what black people do, what men do, what women do. How can we get away from that? There's not much room for us to have free will, but what little we've got of it, we don't know what we want to do with it."

They all had a good laugh. I didn't think it was funny. I scowled at them.

"What about fate? People often say 'it was fated

110

that I meet so and so.'"

"*Nah* sir, depends which parties you go to."
Chanchal again. He thought he was a real comic.

End of lesson and we got lumbered with an essay
on 'Free Will, Fate and Thomas Hardy'. Everyone
gave me nasty looks. I felt like a dart board.

Gazzy and I met by the pond. We shared her
sandwiches, looked at the ducks and didn't talk. For
once we had nothing to talk about.

I had to go to a church hall that the beauty-wallahs
were using for their preparation course. After having
asked twenty different people the directions to it and
getting twenty different answers, I landed in front of
the most massive gothic church I'd ever seen. It was
amazing, it was intimidating. I wondered what Jesus
Christ thought of it.

Cautiously and a little anxiously, I followed a path
that seemed to circle around it, looking for the little
side door I was supposed to find. I'd never been
inside a church before, and the only things going
through my mind were scenes and music from
horror pics. As I looked up at the towers and arches,
I heard the music from *The Omen*. As I passed the
small cemetery on the right I saw hands poking up
through the grass. As I brushed against a bush, I
heard vampire laughter. And it was starting to get
dark. Gulp!

I tried one side door. Locked. Moved on quickly to
see if there was another one. Wished I'd swallowed
my pride and asked that So-and-So to come with me.
Round the corner, light streaming up some steps, an
open door at the bottom. This had to be it! Trying not
to make a sound, for there were no sounds, I crept
down. I listened at the door, put my head around

and looked in. There was a big semi-circular corridor, brightly lit and empty. Here goes!

I followed the curve, my outstretched fingertips trailing a wall. Half-way along I heard faint voices and saw an open door. I tip-toed towards it and peered in. Oh hell, it was O'Driscoll and several others. This must be the multi-cultural Morality Brigade, the Rainbow Coalition of Religions. They all turned round to look at me. I felt sick. I mumbled apologies and was about to turn heel and run when O'Driscoll lumbered towards me.

"What do you want girl? If you want the unholy who trade in flesh, they're round the corner, through the double doors. And tell them girl," following me, as I backed away, "we don't like it, we don't like it one bit! It's faith the world needs, not Roman Circuses, faith and prayer to bring blessings upon the world – Ram-Ram, Allah the Merciful, Sat-Sari-Akal and the blessings of Jesus Christ. There you are, the doors are behind you."

A group of about thirty women were watching Donald and Muck sitting behind a desk, interviewing them all, and giggles and laughter rippled through the group. Varsha saw me and gave a shriek. Oh *Megawd*, had my hair gone white?

She rushed over and gave me a hug, so did Muck, so did Donald. Dear me, aren't I the bees knees!

"I phoned your Mum, told her I'd drop you back home, told her you were our little heroine, we'd never have managed to get this number of women without you. Your article was so sweet and simple..."

"Er...is that a compliment?"

"You dumbo," giving me a little squeeze, "now sit and watch." She took me to the farthest edge of the room, "We're working on interview techniques here, after a while, they'll interview each other. Then in pairs, they'll interview Muck and Don. Separately of course, otherwise we'd be here all night. Muck and Don have a bet on to see how many 'jobs' they can get, they'll be lucky to crawl out of here alive. The photographer from the paper should be coming soon. I think you can put in some real information this time about the preparation, the assertiveness training, the grooming etc. Talk to the women, quote them, write whatever you want. If nothing else, everyone's having fun. Valerie and Jane, have been doing some of the other coaching and they'll be here soon too. So you'll have even more people to talk to. One more thing, make sure you put in that there will be no parade in swimming costumes, and unruly elements will not be tolerated. Time for a break soon. I'm going to get the tea ready."

I pulled her back and told her about the Holy Quartet in the other room. She nodded resignedly and told me there had been rumblings from that quarter, but nobody quite knew what to do about it.

No-one was shy to talk about their lives and as I recorded them on magnetic tape, I got so caught up in just listening I forgot about my list of searching, probing questions.

We were driving home in Varsha's plush deluxe Volvo.

"Most of those women will have to walk home, won't they?"

"Yes, but transport was arranged for anyone living too far away." Varsha threw a few quick looks my way as she braked to a stop at the lights. "What's the matter?"

"You're well set up..."

"I'm comfortable."

I asked her why she got into this whole 'project'.

"Wanted to do my bit, I guess."

"But it won't make much difference, will it? I mean, you have this project. They'll learn things on it and have a Gala Night. A few of them will get jobs through you, but not all, you can't arrange that. Then they'll go back to their council flats or rented places, no jobs, kids to look after, no money. God, I hadn't realised how important money is. I've always worked, didn't have no choice with the kind of parents I got, but then I always had everything too."

I looked down at the little cassette player Suresh had given me, carrying stories, carrying lives. "I've seen people in our supermarkets buying the cheapest things only, and a part of me used to despise them for eating such rubbish. I didn't know then, I didn't know what they have to go through."

I looked out at the shops passing by, loaded with goodies, just inviting people to come in and buy. "Sharon's in terrible debt. She borrowed to buy things for her kids, 'cos she couldn't carry on saying 'No', and then she had to borrow again to pay off what she'd already borrowed. I mean, it's like people in the poorer countries, they get into a spiral and can't get out. She's only doing this for the money, the fees, you lot arranged."

"That's perfectly alright. She doesn't have to do it for anything else."

"But what happens afterwards, and what happens to all the others who never have anything in their lives?"

Varsha glided her car to a smooth stop outside our house.

"Perhaps it's their fault."

My eyes popped out on their stalks. How could she

say that, who wanted to be poor?

"If it's not their fault, perhaps it's fate."

I folded my arms and stared her out. This woman was windin' me up!

"If it's not their fault, and it's not fate, then it must be our fault."

I shook my head indignantly, I'd never taken anything from anyone.

"Look Hari-jan, as you like to call yourself, there are lots of theories about why things are as they are. Reasons to do with history, with economics, with society. We, British Asians, are here because of all those things. Problem is, my little sweetie," getting out and talking to me over the car roof, "finding the solution. I used to think I had it. Imagine me, in my younger days... which weren't that long ago, you little brat, so what if you're as tall as me! Imagine me, skulking around shops, railway stations, public buildings," furtively looking round and skulking up to our front door, "secretly pasting up posters – *Workers of the World Unite, United We Stand, Divided We Fall, Black and White, Unite and Fight,*" on which note she put her finger on our doorbell and forgot to take it off.

Dad came to the door in a right old temper, thinking it was me causing this racket. You've never seen a face change so swiftly. Madam Varsha got invited in for tea and I got kicked into the kitchen to make it.

Late at night, tossing and turning didn't bring any sleep. In the end, I got up and listened to the taped stories of the women again. I listened to stories of women alone, raising children alone, themselves wondering what kind of children they're bringing up in their situations, fathers not paying maintenance.

Stories of alcoholism, of violence, of never being able to get a job that pays a decent wage...

I switched on the computer and started writing. May as well try and make something out of it, since it wouldn't stop whirling round my head. Not to mention the fact that I hadn't done my share of the cooking this week and before long Mum was going to be frying me up in purified ghee.

Looking round at my large room, warm and snug, with its books, cushions, posters, cassette player, I knew I was damn lucky to be where I was, and like Varsha, I felt a need to give back, something, somehow...

When I become a billionaire, I'll buy out the Government, sort out the economy, and the only unemployed will be redundant politicians.

9
WALKING ON GLASS

Aunty Laxmi picked us up after school. He sat in the back and I sat in the front. He didn't talk and neither did I. Aunty Laxmi valiantly kept the conversational flow going, she covered the weather, the news, the neighbour's cat, the economy, the special offers at her supermarket and only faltered when she was within eyesight of her house. The journey certainly hadn't done anything to add to his charm.

Poor Aunty Laxmi must already have begun regretting her invite. I decided to make it up to her and launched into an endless narrative about the pleasures of working in a supermarket, explaining in excruciating detail the intricacies of running such a business, how and why the shelves were organised in the way they were. "Everything is psychologically arranged. It's not food that really runs a supermarket, but psychology."

Aunty Laxmi held up a teapot and coffee jug and silently begged me to choose.

"I love coffee." And then I shut up. Well, I tried. Him, the Omnipotent, had been lounging at the table, lips sealed and glued. If he thought I was going to sit through any more of his home videos, he had another think coming. The table was full with samosas, pastries, cakes, sandwiches, pakoras...

"I told Ma you had a thing about Aloo Pakoras."

Mr Wotsit finally deigning to open his mouth. I busied myself putting out the plates and concentrated on ignoring him.

"She's made stacks, we'll probably have to eat them for the rest of the year."

He was behaving like a real lout, hadn't lifted a finger to help.

Aunty Laxmi was asking whether I liked lots of chilli in my chutney or not. I saw Wotsit, who watched me watching him, pick up two green chillies and bite into them like they were candy. He munched them slowly, savouring the flavour I presume, my poor tongue curled up in protest.

"I think she likes her chutney bland, Ma."

How dare he! I picked up a chilli and, throat screaming in protest, was about to bite into it when he leaned over and grabbed my hand.

"No, don't, you don't have to. They're deadly sharp. I'm used to them, my cousins and I have been having chilli-eating competitions all our lives."

"And getting beaten for it," added Aunty Laxmi, putting the bowl of imli chutney on the table. She looked significantly at our hands, joined together over the long green chilli.

Embarrassment poured over us. He moved his hand. I opened mine, he picked up the chilli. As soon as her back was turned he took tiny bites, looking all the while at me, making it last. Oh heck, my legs were giving way. I collapsed into a chair.

Black steaming coffee poured into my cup. Oh *Megawd*, how am I going to drink that? I looked longingly at the tea I'd spurned.

"Do let me know if it's not strong enough."

I shook my head vigorously, quite positive that I didn't need to have it stronger.

"I hear you outsmarted my son," looking at Suresh with a laugh on her face. "Not only did you get

118

published, you got published in a large circulation newspaper and," pausing for effect, "you got paid for it too."

"You don't have to be so gleeful, Ma."

"Why not? You made an error of judgment. You misread the article, you misjudged Harjinder and I bet you didn't bother to get more information from her. You can get very high-and-mighty, Suresh."

"I don't like being deceived," and this time he wasn't looking at his Mum but staring straight at me.

"You weren't," I retorted hotly.

"And I don't like being..." two-timed was what I was about to say, but suddenly mindful of Aunty Laxmi listening intently, I stopped.

"How about some of this gateau? Now Harjinder, no protests about the size of slice, you're here to enjoy yourself."

Oh really! I raised my eyebrow ironically, just as he was raising his. We looked at each other. Transfixed.

He spluttered into his tea and I spluttered over the mountain of choccy cake and cream being handed to me.

"Anything wrong?" inquired Aunty Laxmi, who didn't seem the dim-witted sort to me.

"Rather a small and stingy portion, Auntiji," I complained aggrieved.

"Hard times, my dear, what to do?" raising her eyes and hands heavenwards, laying on the Authentic Indian Accent. "We even had to sell the pet tortoise, ate us out of house and home."

She's a scream.

A pause, as everyone concentrated on the sugar and cholesterol in front of them.

Aunty Laxmi broke the peace of quiet munching. "Tell me about this beauty contest business."

Was she stirring up trouble deliberately? Did she want to needle her son? Or was she purely after the truth?

"I'm very confused about it," she added by way of explanation.

I glanced over at him. He was giving me his full attention.

I took a deep breath. "Calling it a Beauty Contest was a hook, they thought that there are lots of women who think they're only... only... worth their looks, but you can't make a living on that, and it's the wrong idea for women to have anyway. So Muck, Mukesh that is, and his friends thought up this project of giving women training, but they called it preparation for the Beauty Contest..." I spieled off describing all the different things that were being organised. Muck's name cropped up rather often. "By the end of it, all the women will have earned five hundred pounds each, they don't get it unless they turn up to the preparation sessions. In most beauty contests, the women have to pay a fee to enter. It's the organisers who make the profit, the women are only...cogs in a money-machine."

"What's this about pairing up, English to Asian/ Black etc?"

"To develop co-operation and friendship, and to show...to demonstrate that colour's no barrier and women, mostly have the same problems."

Aunty Laxmi nodded. "It's an interesting idea, they're not making any big claims for it and I'm too old to be a purist. Well, why not? I think we'll go. I'll book the tickets."

"Ma!"

"Yes, my darling son?"

"How far is five hundred pounds going to take

120

those women? It smells of bribery, prettily disguised, but then bribery always is. Where's the money coming from? It adds up to about fifteen thousand pounds."

He was really belligerent. He'd no right to be. I told him, Mukesh had organised it all. He didn't like that, one bit.

"It's not going to make a whit of difference. After all the hoo-ha, the women, shall we call them the contestants, will be exactly back where they were before, no-one's giving them a ticket to riches and fame. It doesn't exist. Proper changes, political changes have to be made if you really want to change the conditions under which women live. This is a stunt, to boost up someone's ego."

"God Almighty," I shook my head. "May I have some more coffee please, Auntiji? Look you," jabbing my finger at him, throwing politeness to the wind, "it's an on-going commitment. There'll be follow up. It's not going to be a one-night wonder and then forgotten about. It's investment in people, in women. Tomorrow night, you come, you watch, you talk to the contestants, you talk to the organisers, then you decide what it's all about."

"I'm not likely to change my mind."

"You're pig-headed."

"You're naive."

"You're wrong."

"You're gullible."

A hand rapped on the table, separated us, brought us back to our sweet, gentle selves.

"Time to have a look at the grass in the garden. Come Harjinder."

Taking my arm Auntiji strolled me out through the French doors. I glanced at Wotsit. He was clearing up.

Auntiji dropped me back home, of course. It was quite nice being chauffeured around. Tradition had its compensations. I thanked her and told her that I really enjoyed myself.

"Hmm. I believe you did." And she raised an eyebrow. I just died.

The next day, I'm singin'-singin' round the swimming pool. Don't know why. But I am. Perhaps it's 'cos Gazzy's decided to join the swimming group again. I don't know what's happened about her heart tribulations. With Gazzy I'm resigned to getting the story in flashback.

She was doing her fifteen laps. I was floating-floating in aqua-pani, flipping my hands and feet, serene on my back, watching the water reflections shimmering on the ceiling.

Madame 'work-till-you-drop-give-me-a-hair-shirt' was clutching the hand rail, gasping, heaving, rasping for breath. I gave her five minutes to recover then gently, delicately, so like a mermaid, floated my silvery (wrong!) dusky delight of a body to her side.

I tickled her. She gave me a whack that had me hitting the bottom. Disorientated in a watery world, trying to breathe, gulping throatfuls of chlorine water. I was too young to die! Survival instinct kick started a movement to the top, then someone was trying to grab me. I was kicking, thrashing...

Someone was pounding my back with a sledgehammer, sprays of water shot out from my mouth. Since when did I become a fountain! Tummy, throat, mouth felt like they had disinfectant swilling around in them... eyes blink, focused on a pair of naked feet, topped by knees bending, towards me. Ugh, vomit rose up through my body to fill my mouth, threatening to drag half my stomach out with it, slithered down over my chin and building up into a little hill right in front of me. Not a pretty sight, not a pretty smell.

"That's good, that's good, chuck it all out."

Thin little fingers closed over my wrist and checked my pulse. Cloths and mops come to wipe up the mess. I tried to rise up, see the flickering circle of faces staring down at me, then my head was pushed back down, a blanket spread over me.

"I'm alright," trying to sit up. I wanted to see what all the drama was about.

"No dear." Head pushed back down, and her hand kept it down. "Now be a good girl and do as you're told. The ambulance won't be long."

"Ambulance!" I shrieked. "I don't need an ambulance!"

"This one's a real toughie. If we let her, she'd probably jump back in and do twenty laps!" Tittering laughter over me.

Not only Mum, but Dad too, came to collect me from the hospital. They rushed in, pale and frightened, smothered me in hugs 'till I couldn't breathe.

"Whose looking after the business?" I asked them. How irresponsible of them both to abandon their duties!

At home I was put to bed, fussed over, coddled, cossetted. I'd dreamed about this, after we'd had some monumental row I'd fantasised about mysteriously dying, with the thought they'll be sorry they treated me so horribly.

Now I was feeling irked, smothered by this non-stop outpouring of love. In the evening I was allowed downstairs. Freedom! Except that I had to lie on the sofa, cushions under me to make me comfortable, a shawl round me to keep me warm.

Gazzy came to see me, a bouquet of flowers in her hand. I was speechless. What was she doing wasting her precious money for?

"I thought I'd killed you."

The most intelligent people could be so stupid sometimes. "Yeah, I can just imagine it. You up on a murder rap, standing in the dock wearing your Hijaab and Jubba. The prosecution launching a brilliant and devastating attack on you, in the middle of which you start doing your nimaz. Mobs outside the courtroom, baying for your blood, you saying, 'She deserved it, your honour' and then there's an everlasting vendetta between our families."

Gazzy didn't think it was funny. "Forget it, it was an accident. And don't I just love all this fuss and attention I'm getting!"

"I let my anger take me over, I wanted to hurt, I wanted to punish."

"Look Gaz, I promise and vow I'll never ever try to tickle you again. Not in the swimming pool anyway!"

She sniffed, tears gathered in her eyes, which she quickly brushed away.

She shocked me. I'm not worth this. "It's alright, Gaz nothing happened, it was an accident." Then I can't stop myself, "You pack a hell of a punch!"

She started sobbing.

I wasn't really the cutie-cuddly type who'd always dole out candyfloss comfort. But this was an extreme situation. I gathered her up in my arms and passed her bunches of tissues.

"You didn't come bobbing back up," speaking thickly through a water-logged voice. "I waited, it must have been just a couple of seconds, but it seemed like hours. I dived in after you. I haven't done lifesaving, so it was a stupid thing to do," shaking her head, "because I just ended up making things worse, I think my interference kept you down longer. The lifeguard gave me a real bollocking afterwards." Scrubbed her face and sat back in her chair. "So did Mrs Anstey. She has to write a report on it."

I told her all these people are silly and she could ignore them.

"Your Mum and Dad haven't said anything to me yet. I'll go and explain to them. You know why it was," twisting and shredding the tissues in her hand, "of course you don't, what's that saying...a woman scorned..."

"Hell hath no fury like a woman scorned," I completed it for her, wondering what was coming.

"That's it. All that agonizing I was doing about my cousin, remember?"

I nodded my head, giving her a little pat.

"It was all unnecessary. I wasn't in the running anyway. Rejected even before the talking began. Mum and Aunty were in the kitchen, he came into my room. At first I thought what's going on, then he started talking, quickly and fast, if they'd seen him there, it would have been really awkward. He said," her voice was really trembly, "he said, we mustn't agree to this marriage business, we weren't really suited, anyway he's in love with someone else and he wasn't going to hurt her." More tears down her face. "Nice of him, wasn't it, to be so honest?"

"Brilliant! Except it would have been twenty times better if he'd had the guts to talk to his Mum first."

"Blokes!" It was a bitter laugh.

"Who needs them!"

10
CENTREPOINT

"All agreed?"

All couldn't care less by this time. The Diwali Planning Committee was in complete disarray. Chanchal and Ivana were writing notes to each other on a pad, while their other hands were getting up to heaven knows what, under the table. Okon was deeply engrossed with the empty playground, he must've seen something very special there. Tom Thumb was in 'Noddyland', though every few seconds he jerked himself awake, giving everyone a Cheshire cat smile, then nodded off again. His life in the fast lane was burning him out.

For some unknown reason Suresh was absent.

"He should have let us know," I complained to Gazzy. "Everyone's supposed to give apologies for absence. This is extremely rude of him."

"Shall we write him a memo, in blood, condemning his deplorable behaviour?" she suggested mischievously.

It's been a while now since our swimming adventure, Gazzy's only just starting to come out of the dumps.

"I'm not wasting a drop of my precious blood on him," I sniffed haughtily. "If anyone has to sacrifice blood it should be him."

"Sacrifice?" Okon suddenly paying attention. "Don't believe in it myself. Quite unscientific."

Gazzy took out her little hammer and banged it six

times, ear-splittingly loud. "All agreed?"

"Yeah!" A thundering roar that had poor little Tom Thumb out of his sleep and off his chair.

"Thank goodness that's over," Gazzy hustling me out. "Hurry up. You're a real slow-coach..."

"That'll do. You got a good brain for words up there. Keep it clean and tidy."

"There's your bus. Two of them. Aren't you lucky!"

"Oh yes. I'm only late for till duty, that's what. If you see me without a scalp tomorrow, you'll know why."

Mum was covering for me at my counter. She gave me a look. A whip would have been kinder. I grovelled. As we changed places she told me that Binny rang, but I may only ring her back after I'd finished my work for the evening.

Was there a national emergency that I haven't heard about? Are we in a war that's cutting off our food supplies? This wasn't supposed to be a busy night. Someone should have told the customers. They were loading up their trolleys like nobody's business. The lean slim look is the 'in' thing, yet these people were buying food like they wanted to be sumo wrestlers. Even Mum was out of her office, restocking the fast-emptying shelves. The skin on my fingers had worn away, I'll never be able to leave finger prints anywhere now.

"Now, make sure you don't make a mistake, dear."

Oh heck, it was the woman to whom I was trying to do a good turn.

"This time I might run off with the loot. Go to the Bahamas for a holiday eh!" sharing the joke with everyone else in the queue.

I glared at her and felt like charging her double.

When we got home, Mum asked if I'd rung Binny yet. I hadn't because it got ever so late by the time we finished.

"She's waiting for it.

"Something's up, that's for sure. Usually, Mum was threatening to put a lock on the phone every time I rang Binny.

Expecting to be assaulted by high-voltage, high-intensity excitement, I held the phone six inches away from my ear, while I waited for her to answer at the other end.

"Hello?"

The reply was low, almost whispered.

At first I didn't even hear it. A horrible dread came over me. It's true you know, you do go cold when you think something quite terrible is about to happen. Had her Marks and Sparks *Kwality Man* done the dirty on her?

"Binny? It's 'Jindi."

She didn't perk up. Said hello again and stopped.

"Mum told me to ring you, seemed urgent like."

"Yeah, it is. I wanted to tell you myself." She sniffed at the other end, blowing her nose. "Did you know that Romi and Kas are coming over from the States?" She stopped, expecting a reply.

I wasn't used to this. She'll carry on in a moment, I told myself. The silence stretched out. This is dreadful. "Really?" I managed to utter. Who says tongues are for talking? Most of the time they have a will of their own. When you don't want them to talk, they talk. When you want them to talk, they don't.

"They'll be here in nine days time. They're stopping over for a few days. On their way to India. That'll be fun, won't it?"

She was doing it again! She was actually waiting

for a reply. I nodded into the phone.

This is the other branch of the family. Mum's and Masi's brother. They live in Denver, and we last saw our cousins about five years ago. They're both teenagers now too and it'll be fantastic seeing them again. We had masses of fun last time we were together.

Strange that I couldn't feel the enthusiasm I should, and Binny was hardly a bag of fireworks tonight.

"They'll be staying with you, 'cos you've got more space." Binny stopped.

I lost patience. Let me have the worst now. It's the waiting, the awful dread that'd do me in. "Binny, don't you have anything more to tell me?"

"Um, yes. Ash and I..."

My eyes closed, hand tightening around the receiver.

"We're getting engaged in twelve days time."

My head whirled. Truly. "How dare you do this to me? You've put me through hell!" I was furious. If she was in front of me, I'd give her a right good shaking. "I thought the worst had happened. Why're you so miserable and grumpy?"

She was trying to interrupt. Well, I wasn't going to let her. "If this is your idea of a joke, it's not funny. You've really upset me. I wouldn't do this to you, put on an act and make you go through agony."

"Jindi, just listen." She was actually laughing. "Shut up! I'm scared. We're both scared. And I've got a really nasty, lousy cold. I've been in bed. Had to take time off work. We were working up to it, then when I heard Romi and Kas and uncle and aunty were going to be here, we decided we may as well do it then, when the whole family is together. I didn't know it would be so frightening. Ash and I talk about it all the time."

She was back to her old self, there's no way I could get a word in now.

"You think about it, deciding to spend your life with another person for the rest of your life. They could change, they could become criminals, they could forget your birthdays, your Christmas presents, they could go off with someone else. The dangers are endless. It's terrifying."

"I'm so glad for you. Congratulations."

Mr God Almighty had deigned to come with me to the 'body market' as he called it. Obliging Mum, obligingly lent him the car. On the way there, he asked me why I had been so adamant in refusing him the first time he'd offered. I couldn't bear to go into that now.

"How's Veronica?"

"We're good friends."

Tell me another one.

"Is that what's been bothering you?"

I shrugged my shoulders. Why should anything bother me?

"Actually it was...um...someone else who I was seeing. Veronica was the cover."

"Huh. You called me gullible once. Well don't you believe it!"

He insisted he was telling the truth.

"Who?" I demanded.

"I can't tell you. It was a secret. She didn't want anyone to know."

"Indian?"

"Possibly."

My mind started zipping through all the girls I knew. There was Mina who was practically Top of the League in everything. Poonum, Madam the Bhangra Dancing Queen, Kamla and Pavan, in my group. Rajinder, Pammi, Jayshree, Sunita, Indira, Meera...

"Stop it."

I looked at him, all innocent like.

"Don't do it. I can hear your mind, whirling round like a computer. It's not important. It's over. It's in the past."

"Why should I believe you?"

"Why should I believe you about your Mukesh, Muck, whatever he is?"

"Because I'm telling the truth."

"Ditto."

I wasn't satisfied, I wasn't happy. I didn't want to believe him. He'd been leading a secret life. What other secrets had he got?

"You don't know how lucky you are," he said. "You got a lot more freedom than most other girls," parking the car by the church hall. "Come on, Cinderella. You don't have to stay in the pumpkin."

Dress Rehearsal. The contestants were going through the Indian Fashion Show bit. Two local Indian boutiques had happily, eagerly, tripped over their feet, in agreeing to advertise their wares. All the English women were going wild over the clothes. Draping dupattas over their faces, jingling bangles on their wrists, clinking anklets around their ankles, tripping around on high-heeled, sequin-embroidered sandles. The Asian women were enjoying it too, but more as connoisseurs, discussing the merits of different styles, dupatta lengths, kameez lengths and colour schemes.

"You know, it's been amazing," Varsha confided in

us with a whisper, "the power relationship has been completely reversed."

I blinked at her, then I got it, it's my Mum's socio-political kind of talk.

"It's the English women who've had to learn how to wear something, how to move in it. They've had to ask for help from women that, two weeks ago they would row with on sight."

"Do you think fashion shows are the key to getting rid of racism in this country?" asked Suresh.

"My dear little boy," she said pityingly, though he was much taller than her, "this is the key for people of different races to enjoy something together. And if it comes to asking questions, I bet I can ask a few that are damn more difficult, than any you could ever think up. You should know, if you don't already, there are different people working in different areas. As for me, I'll carry on with my Harmony Committee. Come with me, let me explain in detail and pour my words of wisdom into your ears."

I'd watched, I'd listened. I'd drunk my cups of tea and was thinking of home and rest when the doors opened. Enter the Morality Brigade. I reached for my tape recorder. Like a phalanx of troopers they stood still, centre stage. Everything around them wound down and stopped. Gabber Singh O'Driscoll stepped forward and delivered a speech of disapproval and condemnation. Muck started to reply, all affability and diplomacy, but didn't get far as the contestants took charge.

"Who are you to tell us what to do?... All you lot want women to do is breed children and scrub the dishes... Some of us don't even have dishes to scrub... Where are you when we need help?... You gonna pay the bills, are you?... I want to better myself, I want my children to respect me... All you want to do is give out charity and you don't even do that... This thing's better than nothing, I can tell you... You lot want women to be slaves.... Who're you to say what God wants?"

It was going great. My tape ran out. The Morality Brigade was battling it out with the punters on the floor. There won't be any winners but it was a good fight. I was about to pour myself another cup of tea when I realised that time was passing pretty fast and it won't be long before Cinderella has to go home.

When time is precious, precious things must be done with it. I pretended to be paying attention to the ding-dong around me, yet it's the boxing match in my mind I was listening to. All the 'Don'ts' I'd been brought up with, slugging it out with the 'Wants' I wanted, refereed by my 'Shoulds' and 'Shouldn'ts'. I thought the Morality Brigade was out there, but it was running rampant in my head.

Do I want to be a Bad Girl? I don't know what that means.

Do I want to be a Good Girl? I don't know what that means either.

Mum said that bargaining in the bazaars of India was the same as what they call 'negotiating' here. "And if you cannot *negotiate* you cannot ever take control of your life." This had been part of her glorious speech to our workforce at the last annual super-duper Christmas Dinner.

OK, I decided, I'm taking charge, because it was up to me to decide, but nothing underhand, nothing secret. I'd 'negotiate', but first I needed to know if I needed to negotiate at all. I looked over at Suresh, eventually he caught my gaze. If he had any nouse he'd get the signal loud and clear. I moved my eyes towards the door.

He's made a move away from the group. I picked up my bag and started to make my goodbyes. Now what? The idiot's stopped at the food table, doing this and that, picked up a plate, put a samosa on it. Oh, he's hungry, is he? Knows I can't afford to take him out to dinner. Telling me he wasn't interested, was he? Fine. I could get a cab. I could forget him. He wasn't everything to me.

He sauntered back to the group and handed the plate to Varsha, then turned round to give me a huge cheeky grin.

We were out. We were laughing. We were waltzing in each other's arms, looking up at a moon spinning faster and faster above us, the dizzying dark dissolving everything between us, feeling feelings I'd never felt before, kisses on kisses, a universe of fireworks sparking.

11
FORKED LIGHTNING

Mum and Dad had a furious row. I got sent upstairs while they battled it out. Feeling awful. I was the devil that brings disaster. I tried to start some work and only ended up doodling on page after page. Odd words, sentences, shoot up from downstairs: "...her sisters never... live with him... no need... gossip..."

Dad wasn't normally given to anger, it's Mum who's the volcano in our house. Now it was him who was shouting and banging the table, Mum answering back, word for word.

Mum had warned me Dad wouldn't like it. She was prepared to concede a certain amount, within strict limits. I realised that Suresh being her friend's son helped more than a little. If it had been someone else, I doubt I would have got her to even consider the idea.

I told Suresh I wasn't prepared to do things in secret. *Joe/Jogesh* Public would have to know. And that meant getting Mum and Dad's grudging consent, approval would have been too much to hope for. Hence the row downstairs, which had started off with me, except it had gone on to get personal between them. Mum said something about a Sandra and Dad retaliated with someone called Raju, Mum exploded and accused him of twisting the truth. That was when I got ordered out.

Gave me something to think about though. You

imagine your parents haven't had a life before 'Beautiful You' arrived on the scene. Old history was pouring out and being fought over downstairs. Wish I had the nerve to go and listen at the keyhole.

Dad and Mum wouldn't speak to each other for days. I became the football in the middle.

"Please ask your mother, Harjinder, to pass the chicken."

"Please tell your father, Harjinder, if he wants the chicken, to reach over and pick it up."

"Please tell your mother, Harjinder, I have suddenly lost my appetite."

"Please tell your father, Harjinder, he needs to lose weight anyway."

I was exhausted. I may as well get married to him. I'd never have the strength to go through this ever again. I rang Aunty Laxmi and told her the whole saga. She was very amused. It made her day. "Who's Raju?" I asked.

"Goodness me, I really couldn't remember. It's happened, you know. Age is catching up on me. 'Bye, 'bye."

Oh yeah? We're invited over for dinner. The excuse being that Suresh's Dad has returned from America and was desperately anxious to make our acquaintance. I got the feeling Aunty Laxmi had been busy behind the scenes. Mum and Dad haven't been talking, didn't talk in the car, but as soon as we got there, it's like someone took a padlock off their tongues and they were behaving like 'The Most Happily Married Couple Of The Year'.

After dinner Aunty Laxmi shooed us out, "The adults need a break from the children. Make yourselves comfy in front of the TV. I'll bring up your coffee."

Dad was longing to object but he couldn't.

Suresh and I didn't utter a sound 'till we're in his loft, the door closed behind us, and then we didn't utter that many sounds either for a while.

"I'd better switch on the TV," he said. "Let go, you vampire." My teeth were having a nice little nibble.

"Don't do it, I'm warning you... I'll retaliate, I'll take my re..."

I moved my lips so he couldn't do any more talking.

The warning bell sounded. We flew apart! Fear brings every cliche alive. He punched the TV switch. It wouldn't work.

"Oh, hell I took off the plug. Over to the desk. Quick."

We sat ourselves down like two regular swots.

"Actually, I wanted to give you this book," he was saying as the door opened.

Aunty Laxmi and Dad have 'come on up', Dad carrying a tray with two cups of coffee on it. "What are you two looking at?" asked Aunty Laxmi as Dad put the tray on the desk. Suresh gave her the book, Anita Desai's "Bye, 'Bye Blackbird'.

"Where on earth did you manage to find it?" exclaimed Aunty L. "I thought it went out of print years ago."

"I know that book," said my Dad.

What an admission! I always thought the only books he bothered with were for book-keeping.

"There's a little poem in here I've often thought about," flicking through the pages. "Let's see if I've remembered it correctly. Here," he put his finger on the page:

"O, England's green and grisly land
I love you as only a Babu can.

137

I used to think," continued Dad.

I was amazed at his talkativeness.

"I used to think it might have been better if she'd written:

O England's green and grisly land,
I love you as only a kala can.

I think she wrote this before the days of the Black Power Movement, before they'd co-opted Black as a word of pride."

Dad laughed when he saw my astonished, astounded, bewildered face. "I'm a lifetime member of the IWA, my dear. The Indian Workers' Association," he explained, seeing my uncomprehending face, "was the first organisation set up by Indian workers. It developed branches all over the country. This was all before the days of the CREs, the community workers, the race workers, the equality workers. I haven't always been this single-minded, money-minded business man."

"Is that all?" said Aunty Laxmi, in an Indian gesture of surprise. "You are too modest of yourself, Amrik bhai."

Everyone smiled, amused, then Dad looked a little sad, looking at me, saying he wished he'd spent more time with the children.

I jumped at him and gave him a huge tight bear hug.

"Look at her," he said. "She's taller than I am."

12
THE WORD

"It's out," was the first thing Gazzy said to me, as I skidded to a stop, by the school gate. "Follow me," she commanded.

I was tired, I was hungry, I was overloaded with excess baggage. And Gazzy reckoned she was going to set a new record for the one minute mile. Plus carrying on one of those multi-ethnic conversations jumbling up Panjabi, English, Urdu and any other lingo-bingo that happened to flit through her mind. Throwing bunches of sentences over her shoulder at me, she whizzed through traffic and people.

Mum was clamping down on me tighter than a vice these days. It seemed like because she'd agreed to let me see Suresh, she had to compensate by tightening up in every other area, the latest thing being saris. Time I learnt to wear them, I was told, and 'enjoy it too', as said through gritted teeth. How was it that such an essential part of my education had been neglected? She blamed herself of course, she had been too busy working – working to pay the bills, put food in the fridge and buy us our consumer durables. She would make up for it now.

Gazzy had been her tool. Deliberately or not, I'll never know.

"There's no problem in getting sari blouses and petticoats stitched," she'd said, and told them (Aunty Laxmi was round too, delivering her Diwali invite) about a Pakistani tailor who'd just set up in business.

The two of them, Mum and Aunty L, went a teeny-weeny bit wild. I wondered if there was something in the biscuits they'd been nibbling.

"A real Desi tailor?" they questioned her, acting like they'd just discovered treasure and couldn't believe it.

"Proper home-trained? ...Knowing all latest designs? ... Imagine that!" they said to each other, wide-eyed. "Remember Ramprakash on Connaught Road?"

Have you ever seen two perfectly mature, grown-up mothers giggle like schoolgirls at some smutty joke?

"Indeed, yes," said Aunty L mischievously, "most certainly, Harjinder must have her blouses stitched and her petticoats done..." then they were off again.

So there I was, their couture courier, with bundles of materials, measurements, style specifications, and orders to get him to do this, that and everything else.

Gazzy had stopped on the steps of a terraced house, waiting for me to catch up with her. I was tired, I was hungry, and now I was exhausted and badly bad-tempered.

"What are you going to do?" she asked, before I even got a chance to get my breath back.

I just leaned against the wall, shaking my head. She must have taken that for an answer, because she shook hers too, slowly, sadly.

I just exploded. It seemed like I spent my whole life walking on some tight-rope and here she was shaking her head at me like I was the lowest of the low. "Look Gaz, I know I'm not good enough for you. I'm always getting myself into a mess, running round like a headless chicken...But don't you look at me like I'm some kind of criminal. I haven't done nothing," banging my fist on the wall for emphasis. Scraped all the skin off.

Not an ounce of sympathy from her. She just looked harder and sterner.

"Being your friend doesn't mean I have to like everything you do. And now that everything's come full circle I don't know what you can do. You don't know what you can do. All I can do is be your friend."

"Don't bother."

"Don't be so stupid. Some people just can't be helped. Well I've told you. I've done my duty. Now it's up to you."

The door opened behind us. They must have heard us shouting. Two women came out, carrying bags, smiling and satisfied. We were ushered in by Madam Wife, clipboard in hand, biro behind her ear, paan in her mouth.

"I have tried chewing-gum," she said as she offered us paan while we waited. "We were in Amrika, and there they all do it," ticking off our names on her clipboard. "But it was terrible, terrible thing, artificial colour, artificial taste. My husband is with client. Please have refreshments as you wait, tea and coffee machines over there. No money. Press button only. Here is a leaflet about our fashion house," handing us a glossy folded thing.

Gazzy and I looked at each other, this was unbelievable. I'd accompanied my mother and aunt on 'stitching' expeditions before where we usually landed up at the home of some woman who did it as a part-time job. We'd never come across anything like this before.

"Now let me tell you about my husband," said Mrs

Tailor confidentially, sitting down near us.

Gaz and I don't even bother to look at each other. What's coming now?

"My husband is an artist." She stopped.

We were impressed.

"He will take your orders, but he must also exercise his artistic freedom. If something will not work, he will say so, if something needs to be done differently he will say so. It is better to be clear before cloth is cut. You understand? Please say if this is agreeable to you."

I nodded my head enthusiastically. I was going to be stitched up by a Rembrandt.

My Rembrandt was several years older than his wife and several inches shorter than myself. He asked me to stand by the French windows and walking around me, looked me up and down, and every way around. I began to understand all that giggling. Thank God, Gaz and his wife were here.

"Please remove all loose clothing," taking up a tape measure.

I looked around desperately. His wife snorted sarcastically.

"He cannot take your measurements unless you remove those twenty layers of clothing that you are wearing. Do you want a sari blouse or a parachute?"

Reluctantly, I started to take off a jumper.

"Your details will be entered into our computer and next time you will not have to have such a long consultation." She was armed with her clipboard and biro. "T-Shirt off too please."

This woman would have made a great sergeant major. I complied. However, I decided I hated my mother.

The tape measure got to work, measuring and

cataloguing every bulge, pimple and dip. He shouted out centimetres, she scribbled them down, I tucked in my tum, she told me off. I peeked at her pad and saw myself as columns of numbers. If they ever need to build a Bionic version of me, they'll know where to come!

He looked at the saris I'd brought and picked up the one I've christened 'Starlight Express'. It's dark blue with a huge silver border and silver bits sprinkled through.

"This is a fun one to start with, yes?"

He's coming at me with the tape measure again.

"How sexy?"

"What!" My voice came out as a long, thin squeak.

"This is for evening wear, yes? You must tell me your intentions so that I may translate into design."

He saw me looking at him, speechless, flabbergasted.

"You are Modern Western Girl. Of course, I may speak to you like this. The other ladies, they do not mind. They are very amused."

I still didn't reply, he looked at his wife for guidance. She shrugged her shoulders. She'd given up on me.

"Did you do this...ask this...this kind of thing in Pakistan?" I managed to croak out.

He gave a smile of pure nostalgia and longing. "Back home, things are said. When they are not said, words are like a rose, the petals soft and delicate, each petal different from the other." He sighed looking down at his tape measure. "We will see what we can do, and cheat Mummy's watching eyes. The neckline," his tape measure plunging deeper than I've ever allowed the sun to peep, "the length, up to here."

"That's too short," I protested.

"No, no, you see the sari has a beautiful border, magnificent, you must show it off."

"Must I?" He wasn't going to hear a word I said.

"All set?" asked Gaz as we walked back.

I couldn't reply. I was in an exhausted daze. I asked her what she's going to wear to the Diwali Do.

She contrived to look mysterious. "Wait and see. You," jabbing me with her finger, "you've got to work out how you're going to deal with your drama. This is serious. The lids off."

I squealed with delight, then clamped a hand over my mouth. Gotta be cool. My Drama had just driven up, gotten out and opened the door for us.

13
FIREWORKS

"You're not!" she stared horrified at my footgear, peeping outrageously from under the hem of my sari.

Tonight, for the *Booty Contest*, I chose a creation in pale pink lilac, printed over with shadow flowers that glittered subtly in the light. "It's the fashion. Everyone's doing it." Tomorrow night for the school's Diwali Do, I shall glorify myself in 'Starlight Express'.

"I must be paying for the sins of a past life."

"And Harjinder will pay in the next life. Out!" Dad was in charge tonight.

He was meeting his favourite daughter and son-in-law and he wasn't going to let our fashion and philosophy debate hold him back.

Oh, oh, trouble at the entrance. The Morality Brigade got here first. They were stopping everybody who was going in, giving them leaflets and lectures. My heart sank as we got near them. They've probably turned away half the audience! I tried to hustle Mum and Dad along the outskirts hoping to escape them, but nothing doing as the Clean-Sweep-Caretaker saw me and made a bee-line for us.

"Good to see you, good to see you. Very good work."

Oh really!

"Here's a leaflet about our community initiative."

He was standing right in front of us so we could

hardly sidestep. "Religion, the meaning of religion is about fighting injustice and evil today, on our doorsteps. Come to our 'Day for Suffering', there are the details," pointing to the print that I was too dazed to read. "Good Samaritans, that's what we all need to be. Every day in every way. Enjoy the show."

I was confused, in every way I could be.

Kemal and Bobby were waiting in the foyer. These two are every parents dream come true. I hung back in all the hubbub of greeting, hugging and exclaiming that went on. Dad gave Bobby (my B-i-L as I call him) hearty slaps on the back. B-i-L didn't seem to mind at all. Must be an ancient male ritual.

I looked around wondering if God Almighty would deign to make an appearance. He'd kept teasing me right to the last minute with his may-be he will and may-be he won't. 'Till I'd told him I couldn't care less. I went over to the hall entrance and peeped in. Perhaps he got here early.

"I thought I recognised that inquiring little nose," Muck, mucking around as usual. "Like the arrangements?" They've divided the room in two. Men on one side, women on the other. "Isolate potential trouble makers, minimise disturbance, maximise damage limitation. My strategy," he smiled smugly.

"Excellent work my boy," I patted him on the back, not very gently, trying out the old male ritual. He couldn't be in on it, the coward tried to dodge me. I showed him the leaflet. "Explain, please," I begged.

"Good, isn't it? Nothing to do with us. As you know the contestants, the clients, call them what you will, had a bit of a word with them, remember? It seems to have caused a slight shift in their modus operandi. They're still breathing hell, fire and damnation but they seem to have added another prong to their fork. They're going to work with us on the follow-up."

"Rather sudden," I observed dryly.

"When one of the women said 'if you got mould on the walls and leaky windows no amount of praying to God will fix them'. 'Yes he can,' said Mr Singh from the Gurudwara, and promised to send round a carpenter. You know what it is?" lowering his voice and almost whispering in my ear. "The God-wallahs reckon they found themselves a ready-made congregation."

"Enjoying yourselves?"

His Majesty in person. I blinked in amazement, so dazzled by a white ironed shirt, black tie and dinner jacket, I missed the sharpness in his voice.

"I've started so I'll finish..." Muck went on. "When they started damning the iniquities of this day-and-age: violence, drugs, alchohol et al. Unanimous agreement! You should've hung around a little longer. You'd have been knocked backwards. Now, back to the business of living, my tickets for tomorrow night?" cupping his hands into a begging bowl.

"Money first."

"That's all you think about," he complained, rummaging around in his pockets and eventually bringing out a wallet. "American Express?" Dead cheeky like, expecting me to say you-know-what.

I coolly lifted the card from his fingers, popped it into my purse and walked off with Suresh.

Mum was coming over to us, looking quite cross-eyed. I moved two feet away from Suresh and pretended we were nodding acquaintances. Varsha, she informed, had requested my presence at the front door. I dashed off quick. I love to oblige.

Outside, Varsha and the Morality Brigade were deep in conversation. Life is so unpredictable, I thought. You never know who's going to get pally with whom!

"You missed the action I'm afraid," Varsha consoled me. "Pity, because you might have been able to identify some of them." Apparently, some of the youths who paraded themselves as members of some war-hungry gang had turned up and been given a short, sharp, shock by our very own Morality Brigade.

"They are just like lost children," said Mr Purewal, "they need someone to give them good guidance and a good telling off."

"Which you all did superbly," Varsha laughed, "you should've heard the argy-bargy out here."

I felt like wringing my hands in despair. I'd missed the event of the evening. At least I'd better not miss the show.

Inside, the women all buzzed and chattered, English and Asian getting all mixed up together. Looking around I could see that there was a difference in their behaviour, now that all the men had been herded off to the other side, rather more of the ingredients of relaxation and conviviality. Strange. Gives one something to think about, and I was thinking about it, when I heard my name echoing all over the hall. People clapped, my mother pushed me off my chair and Varsha gestured madly from the stage.

"Go on, you dumbo," hissed my sister Kemal.

She's such a sweetie!

I didn't know what was going on, but it seemed like I had to go up, that's what everyone else seemed to want me to do. You ever walked in your sleep? I haven't. But I now know what it's like.

I got to the stage, climbed up the steps at the side and nearly staggered back when Varsha faced me with a gigantic bouquet of flowers. Shouts of 'speech, speech,' rang out.

"Do you want to say a few words?" she whispered in my ear while pretending to give me a peck on the cheek.

I shook my head, but did stop to give a star-studded smile and wave to everyone. My fans!

The rest of the evening passed in a haze, as we were all caught up in the razzamatazz of a show-business event. It was really quite excellent. The whole thing worked! Women who'd never stood up in front of an audience (some who'd never been able to stand up for themselves) were doing presentations, reading out small speeches (well spiced with ironic little barbs), dramatically and flamboyantly showing off in the fashion show, followed by the select few who'd decided to air their singing talents. Each act aroused loud and generous applause. It was an audience that wanted to be pleased and pleased they were, especially when Tracey and Sharan-jeet did a Bhangra number, Tracey's few lines of Panjabi wowing the audience crazy. Watch out Apache Indian!

I was beginning to relax and thinking to myself that their 'project' had actually worked. Phase number one successfully completed, when loud shouts and a scuffle on the men's side rudely interrupted the flow...

"Crazy bitch, mad cow.." and other such endearments rang out before the voice was muffled, scattering the two women on the stage into the shadows.

The audience craned their heads and ears backwards to hear what was happening, when Madam Varsha, the ever-efficient emollient took to the stage, and brought the audience back into the palm of her hand. The woman is a natural for show-biz!

"Relax folks," Varsha back on the stage, calming everyone. "We have a joker in the audience. He is being assured that we are not amused. Please greet the next act..."

There was another quick, small scuffle on the men's side, then we saw someone being escorted out.

"Now if you were a *real* newshound," taunted my sister Kemal, "you'd be after them like a shot, hot on the pursuit of a scoop."

I popped a peanut into my mouth and smiled at her so condescendingly, it was a real pleasure.

"I already know all about it." I let a decent interval elapse, then murmured something about going to the loo.

Police in the foyer! They weren't supposed to get this heavy. Don and Muck were supposed to take care of any little incidents. This was unfair and over the top. How dare they call the police in! Don saw me and came over.

"They're only kids," I flared out at him, "you're not supposed to be..."

"Calm down. It's nothing to do with that," moving me away towards a corner, speaking almost in a whisper. "It was a man armed with a knife. Several knives in fact. The maniac was out to do his wife some real damage. She's one of the contestants. We're damn lucky no-one got hurt. We'd packed the blokes side with our friends and briefed them to watch everyone. They were on the look out for your little tricksters, one of them was sharp enough to spot this chappie as he was about to do his knife throwing act."

I looked behind me. There was a sofa. I collapsed onto it.

I didn't have a good night's sleep and Saturday night hit me before I'd even had a shower. Gazzy rang to make sure I was ready. The speed with which I got myself geared up in my 'Starlight Express' would have been a credit to any quick-change artist. The blouse was much too small. That devious, designing tailor! I tugged and stretched and pulled uselessly.

Wrapping a shawl around me I tripped downstairs, and nearly tripped down the stairs. My sister Kemal, who'd come to stay the night, was passing on the stairs, and had a good laugh as I clung on to the banisters.

"Walk, before you run!"

I had to be there early so Dad gave me a lift. Picking up the front of my sari, no time for elegant entrances, I dashed into the school hall and found the Diwali Committee seated round a table, scoffing samosas and suchlike.

"But we've got to get ready! What are you all doing?"

"Look around you, Cinderella," said Mr Suresh Richardson, taking my arm, for a tour around the hall. The decorations were up, the tables were out, the bar (soft drinks only) ready to go. Even the sound system was in perfect order, the music gear all out on the stage, a babble of voices from the dressing rooms behind the stage.

"What do you think," he asked, as we found ourselves in a shadowy niche, "of my organisation?"

"To tell you the truth," I murmured, drawing my sari over his head, "I don't really want to think about anything." So we didn't.

"Excuse me please," a very polite voice behind us.

Suresh quickly moved away.

I couldn't quite make out who it was in the shadows. A figure, with an armful of clothes walked between us. Reaching the edge of the stage where the light from the hall filtered through, she looked back. It was Shakuntala-the-shadow.

"Peeping Tom," I muttered. Suresh started back out. I caught his arm. "What's the hurry?"

"What's the hurry! There are people to be organised for the car park, the tickets, the stewards..."

"Why are you so angry?"

He stopped. His back towards me. Then he turned and gave me a hug.

Goodness, that was unexpected!

"There are still some details to tidy up. Come on, let's go," holding out his hand.

The group round the samosa table was silent and staring at the door. What's happened? Thoughts of last night flashed into my mind. Then I saw who they were staring at. A gorgeously dressed creature, in a purple and gold kameez, with a full golden shalwar, wearing a turban of intertwined colours, a half-veil, hooked across her face. Gazzy!

I put my fingers in my mouth and wolf-whistled. That broke the spell! Gaz shook a fist at me. Definitely not a turn-the-other- cheek type is she?

The families started filtering in, not only mammas

and pappas, but grandpappas and grandmammas, little ones, middle ones, infant ones. The whole shabang! The girls dressed to kill, the guys sticking in groups, more than ready to be murdered, inviting danger, throwing out oblique, indirect, yet clear to read signals. The dads prowling round with shot-gun eyes. This was going to be a night to remember.

The Bhangra group came bouncing onto the stage, and announced that the first numbers were for the 'respected elders' who really knew how to Bhangra-Boogie and the kids to keep off the floor, if you please.

My heart sank as I circled round with my tray picking up empties. That's really going to get the joint jumping, is it?

They were half-way through their number, and that was with the singer repeating and doubling up on lines, and not a sign of a soul on the floor. 'I told you so', ready on my lips, though I hadn't told them any such thing, silly stupid idiots prancing round on the stage. We didn't hire them to sink the show, they've burst the bubble before it's even had a chance to bounce, when to my great surprise (and I must say, eventual delight), a grandpappa and a grandmamma got on the floor and started doing their stuff.

I've never heard so much noise, everyone was up, clapping and shouting. The special effects department released their smoke clouds, the strobe lights got going, and by the time the number finished there were half-a-dozen couples demonstrating the pukka, authentic Bhangra as it used to be danced in their day. The mammas and pappas got a go next, but there was no keeping the rest of the extended family out any more, as the seniors, juniors and kids who ain't even out of kindergarten yet, muscled in.

I looked at the Bhangra group with new respect. I'll have to do an article on them. When I'm Editor, that is. When I've won the elections for the editorship, that is. When that So-and-So has cleared off. He wasn't getting the chance to turn down any more of my masterpieces. I'd asked Gazzy to be my campaign manager, she was humming and hawing, playing hard to get. I'll just have to give her an ultimatum. After her, I've got a second possibility, Jamie's been hovering around as the second choice.

With the show safely on the floor, I got busy clearing the tables, carrying away trays of empty glasses and gathering up the paper plates, when Mr Wotsit came along, took the tray from me and lifted an eyebrow.

"Wanna check out my style?"

I could lift my eyebrow too. "I really don't think I want to be bored."

But somehow it happened and we ended up on the dance floor.

"I learnt mine in India," he boasted, leaning forward, shouting into my ear.

What a show-off! I shook my head, showing him I didn't hear a word, turning my back on him. He worked his way round to my side and without even trying, we worked out a little routine. Felt neat, being in step. Someone bumped into me. I looked around and it was that Peeping Tom Shakuntala. I'd begun to wonder about her.

Interval.

The band went off to rest their throats, the people sat down to rest their feet, the bar and food tables got busy serving and dishing. Okon and Tom Thumb moved parts of the stage round, ready for the fashion show. There *had* to be a fashion show. Everyone's addicted to fashion. It's much healthier than Crack or Ecstasy.

I was running backwards and forwards, doing my Super-Waitress bit, trying not to get stains on my sari, scolding myself for my vanity in wearing it. And wondering about blessed Ivana. The blessed Ivana who was supposed to be doing half this work!

VT Rice materialised at my side. I touched her to make sure she was real.

"How'd you get here?"

"I caught the number fifty six bus and walked here from the bus stop. I went through the corridor at the back and into the dressing rooms behind the stage..."

I congratulated her on her journeys, and went to another table to fill my tray. Coming back to the bar, she was still there, exactly where I left her. She watched me unload my tray. The lights were dimming, gentle introductory music starting to fill the space, quietening the crowd.

"Hari-jan," her voice sounded different, "come with me for a few minutes."

I was about to protest and point to the amount of work ready-and-waiting when the tone of her voice and the look on her face, told me this was no time to argue.

I nodded and followed her, a cold, icy feeling in me. She led me out of the building, across the little playground to the car park area. Three people were standing under a wall light. Gazzy, Suresh and of course it had to be, Shakuntala.

VT's heels clicking on the tarmac, my Reeboks making a muffled crunching sound. For a while no-one said anything. I looked at Gazzy, she looked away. Suresh stared back at me, hard and unblinking. Shakuntala was standing against the wall, arms folded, moving grit backwards and forwards with her feet. VT Rice went to stand next to her.

"Is it true?"

"Is what true?" I asked in return. I wasn't stalling. I needed to be quite certain what the question was.

"Don't play games with me."

"I'm not."

"Veronica. Why don't you remind her?" Shakuntala, no longer the shadow but the 'Acid Queen'.

"OK. Hari-jan, we made a bet by the pond, that you would get him, Suresh, make him your boyfriend. That's true, isn't it?"

"Yes."

"And Gazzy witnessed it. Didn't you, Gaz?"

"Yes, but..."

"So it's true?"

He always wanted to hammer home the point.

"Yes, but..."

"Excellent!" Suresh, being hale and hearty. "How flattering! Except it's not. And it's women who're always complaining about being seen as objects. There's certainly more to you than meets the eye. Do we say, well played? And I believe there's a built in forfeit too, you even worked out the finer details. Enjoy your victory to the full, Hari-jan. Let's do the forfeit as well."

Even a sentenced man is allowed a last request. I touched his arm, he moved it away. "It wasn't like that." I made an effort to control my wobbling, put all my strength and conviction into my voice. "It's not true. I didn't start seeing you just to win a bet. At first I tried to keep away from you, and then after a

156

while I didn't want to give you up." I hated having to talk like this, especially in front of an audience.

"True love got the better of you, did it?"

Ghastlier and ghastlier!

"Why didn't you tell me?"

"I tried." How to explain my pathetic little efforts? "It didn't have anything to do with you. It was a stupid conversation between Veronica and me. I never took it seriously."

"It was serious enough to split us," Shakuntala, still glued to the wall, throwing out darts of venom.

"I didn't know about you."

"I doubt if it would have made any difference. You don't care what you do to other people!"

"That's not fair," Gazzy striding over and standing by my side. "She didn't have a secret hide-it-in-a-hole thing with him. She did it honestly, openly..."

"She flaunted it!"

"You encouraged it. Don't forget I'm a witness. What were you trying to prove?"

"Listen, everybody," Suresh, holding up his hands, trying to calm everyone down. "This is between me and Hari-jan."

"No," Shakuntala finally leaving the wall and coming forward, "this is between me and her. She came between you and me, she split us up!"

"I don't think so. If you want the truth, I don't think we would have lasted much longer. Perhaps you suspected it."

Shocked, Shakuntala moved back a step, her hand searching for the support of the wall behind her. "After all the risks I took for you. You know what my father's like, he would have beaten me to hell and back. All the lies I told you, Veronica covering up for us, how can you say that? How dare you!"

In a quick, swift movement, she was in front of him, arm swinging up in an arc, cracking across his face. He fell, hitting the ground with a horrible thud. She stood over him, pure rage steaming out, catching me as I rushed forward. "Rich little bitch, all you had to do was lift a finger and he went running to you. Well one day, he'll do it to you. Someone else will come along, she'll lift her finger and he'll go running after her. Then you'll know what it feels like," tears streaming down her face.

Veronica put her arms around Shakuntala's shoulders and led her away. Gazzy helped Suresh to sit up, then ran after the other two.

Blood on his shirt, on his face. He dabbed at it with a tissue. I knelt down, looking at him, trying to work out the damage.

"It's a nose bleed," I said, stating the obvious.

"Yes. Have you got any more tissues?"

I shook my head. I hadn't come expecting something like this.

"Aren't you supposed to tear up your sari and use it to make bandages?"

"It's expensive."

He nodded his head understandingly.

"We could tear up your shirt," I suggested helpfully.

"Can't. Sentimental value. Someone special gave it to me," peeping at me from under his eyes.

What's he mean by that! He needed a good sorting out, he did. "Perhaps you'd better get some first aid. Do you want some help?" I managed to heave him up.

He stumbled a bit, barging into me, nearly sending both of us flying this time. Pulling one arm across my shoulders and putting my other one round his waist, we hobbled towards the main building.

"You know," he said quietly, and I waited in anticipation, thinking he's about to make some profound comment on this evening's drama, "you've never worn anything so very interesting, before. My compliments to the tailor."

I stopped still and looked at him.

"All this time, I've been lugging you across this lousy tarmac, you've been gazing, you've been..." trying to find the right words, "you've been sexually exploiting me!" I dropped him like a dead weight and marched off.

"Didn't you ever want to win the bet?"

It was like an arrow in my back. I think Shakuntala had the right idea. I returned, he was sitting on the ground, now nursing an ankle.

"I think it's broken. I landed awkwardly."

"Poor you. I'll go call the emergency services and have a helicopter ferry you out. And yes, everything I did was to win the bet."

"Well I used you to get rid of Shakuntala."

"No, you didn't."

"Yes I did."

"You're horrible."

"So are you."

Suddenly he'd pulled me down and we were rolling around on the ground. My sari was going to be ruined.

"Hari-jan. Hari! Your Dad's here," Gazzy in the doorway. "Hurry up, he's looking for you."

What would I do without her?

14
BUBBLE AND SQUEAK

We've been invaded. The Americans have landed and are lording it over us. According to them, our house was just so cute, tiny and petite, they wondered how we don't go bumping into each other all the time. Our fridge just freaked them out. How can a whole family live out of such a teeny-weeny titchy thing? They all took it in turns to go and have a peek. I felt affronted, I informed them our fridge was pretty giant-size for England. That was a mistake. They shrieked and exclaimed at each other, 'If this is big, how small are the rest?' They trooped back in to examine the contents. So little choice! How can we possibly live like this?

How can they talk so loud all the time? I thought. The neighbours will be round in five seconds flat at this rate, even though ours is a fully detached Des-Res and conversation doesn't normally carry from one wall to the next. And to think I'd actually been looking forward to their visit, but my cousins have grown up and gone completely Americana ga-ga.

You know about Americans making jokes about English roads? Sure enough these Yanks had to have their say too. Not only that, they then start complaining about the number of people who walk. 'How come they aren't driving?' they want to know. They went on a shopping trip to see the local flora and fauna, ending up with a visit to Masi's house. They came back pale and quiet. Cat got their tongues at last. Good!

'What terrible poverty!', they complained. 'And the English people are real dirty and unhealthy-looking'. 'Is it true they don't have showers in their houses?' The terrible racism here is worse than anything else, they never get that in the States. They really can't understand why we've stayed here all this time.

"They're my racists, leave them alone." I felt like going out and buying a Union Jack. I could criticise England, I lived here. I could criticise the people, I had to deal with them day after day. I could hate the English for their narrow bigoted minds. But these horrible twangy foreigners had no right. Go back Yank is what I thought.

I called Suresh and asked him to come over. I was at the end of my patience, energy and good manners. The Yanks went goggle-eyed when Mum told them he's my boyfriend. She'd never used that word before, but I reckon they were getting to her too, so she was doing her bit of flaunting and showing them how 'modern we are'. I wondered why they rushed off upstairs.

Aunty L drove him round. Cossetted brat. Can't he even bring himself to turn the ignition key these days. He hobbled around the car towards our door. One heavily bandaged foot lifted off the ground, the rest of him leaning on a walking stick.

"Broken?" I asked hopefully. That was my doing!

He shook his head. "Do you think you could help me over the step, please?"

I took his arm, he leaned all his weight on me, the twerp.

The Yanks slithered down, wearing dresses, lipstick and perfume. How gross! Why can't they disappear now? Beam them back, Bush. Mum invited Aunty L and Suresh to Binny's engagement party, to be held at our house, on the morrow. That reminded me, Binny hadn't rung me to discuss her wardrobe yet. I'd better give her a tinkle, later.

The transatlantic Uncle and Auntie bemoaned the fact that Binny hadn't asked them to husband-hunt for her in the US of A.

"Such a match, I would have arranged," said my aunt proudly. "Properly qualified professional with house, car, swimming pool. Minimum. And what will she get here? Very sad business. Harjinder. When you are ready," she turned on me, "you come and stay with us, we'll see you're properly fixed up."

They really are insufferable!

Binny's day dawned early ie I get woken up even earlier than normal, to help my Dad shift some furniture around, organise the food and drinks table while Mum went off to fetch everything from the caterers. The Mississippi Belles were still enjoying their beauty sleep. Masi and Binny arrived with a whole suitcase of stuff. I lugged it upstairs for Binny, put a clean towel in the bathroom for her and asked her if she wanted any help in choosing her clothes.

"Ta, 'Jindi," looking at herself in the mirror, taking out bottles, jars, pots, a whole cosmetic counter. "I've already sorted it out with Ash. We've co-ordinated."

"Do you talk to him a lot?" I asked, hovering by the door.

"All the time. The light's not very good around your dressing table, is it?"

"Sorry."

I wandered out into our garden, where we've got a tiny little pond, put in by the last owners. That's where Gazzy finds me. "Little fishes in a little pond. A lot's happened to them, hasn't it?"

"Don't be sad," she said.

162

"I'm happy too. It's a mixture of both."

A knock on the French doors. Suresh and his walking stick. I broke his ankle, I think again, I don't know why. Gaz and I run back, shivering. Hadn't realised it was so cold.

"There she is, sir," Suresh pointing his stick at me, speaking to Mukesh.

What's he doing here?

"No need to be lenient with her, she's a confirmed tough nut."

"Want your other ankle broken?"

"See what I mean. You've got something that belongs to my friend here."

"No I haven't," I started to say, then remembered a blue plastic card. Oh, hell! Now where had I put it? Binny was upstairs, the whole room would be in chaos.

"Trade you my Reeboks for it," I suggested brightly, hoping to at least get a laugh from everyone.

"Done." He's sitting down, unlacing his shoes.

I'd forgotten what a contrary little sod he is. Taking a deep breath, I fetched my prized possessions. They fit him perfectly. He's fairly small and I'm fairly tall. Looking at them on his feet, watching them do little dance steps and twirls, it's quite clear that they've found a new home.

"They're nearly here," shouted my Dad, putting down the phone. He'd organised a look-out with a neighbour two streets away. There's a hurry-and-a-scurry as everyone gets into place, the Granthi, calmly sitting behind the holy book. Masi, my parents, uncles and aunts lined up behind me. I'm standing at the door, a silver jug of water in my hand for the Saghan, a pink dupatta on my head and bare feet wriggling on the doormat.

I sneaked a look back, Gazzy is perched near the window, half-turned towards everyone, half-turned away from everyone. Suresh catches me peeking and lifts an eyebrow. Mine twitches in response.

"They're here," everyone whispers behind me, quite unnecessarily as three cars drive in. And would you believe it! They're all jostling from the back, wanting to be the first to get a sighting of Binny's Marks and Spencer's *Kwality Man*. I glared at them sternly. It's my duty to be the first to greet him. So says tradition. They had better remember that.

Oh my! What is this vision in a cream silk kurta, seemingly floating towards me? Binny had been mingy with her words, that's for sure. I take a deep breath, fortify myself with the thought that I have already spoken for another (sort of, if you see what I mean) and gracefully, elegantly, bend down to pour water at the sides of the steps. The vision pours a stream of pound coins into the jug. They're mine! That's tradition!

Glossary of Asian Words and Phrases in Text

acha	– meaning 'yes', 'I understand', 'alright'
Allah	– the Islamic name for God
aloo	– potatoes
Amma	– reference to mother in Muslim cultures
Angrezi	– the English language
ashram	– religious retreat
atta	– dough, used for making chappattis
babu	– respectful name for male elder eg father, brother
bachas	– children
bas	– finished, enough
beti	– affectionate term for young girl
bhai	– brother
Bhangra	– Panjabi music, now popular amongst many Asian young people
Bharat	– referring to India as a great nation
bhindi	– okra or 'ladies fingers'
bilkul	– totally
bukwaas	– rubbish, gossip
chacha	– uncle
'Chal Akela'	– words from a well known Indian song, meaning 'Walk Alone'
chamchas	– crawlers, fans, sychophants
chai	– tea
chappels	– Indian sandels

churidaars	– tight drain–pipe trousers, worn with a kurta
dadima	– father's mother
desi	– traditionally Indian
dhanyia	– coriander
divas	– small clay lamps lit in religious ceremonies
Diwali	– the celebration of Ram's return from exile
dupatta	– scarf worn with shalwar kameez
Eid	– annual Muslim festival (for Ramadan or pilgrimage to Mecca)
ghee	– clarified butter
gobi ke paratha	– cauliflower filled chapatti
gorah	– white male
Granthi	– Sikh priest
Guru	– respected teacher
Guruji	– in this context, The Almighty
Gurudwara	– Sikh temple
gulab jamuns	– Indian sweets, filled with syrup
gup–shup	– chit–chat
hain	– a questioning exclamation, usually meaning 'what?'
Hanuman	– see Ramayan
harami	– bastard
Hari–jan	– a term coined by Mahatma Gandhi meaning 'Children of God' in reference to the lowest Indian caste, the 'Untouchables'
Hijaab	– a headscarf or veil worn with a cloak
Jantramantra	– an act of wizardry, magic word similar to 'abracadabra'

Jhansi ki Rani	– the Queen of the kingdom of Jhansi, who led a rebellion against British rule
jubba	– headscarf
jungly	– wild, unruly
imli	– fruit of tamarind
kala	– an Afro–Caribbean/African man
khadi	– raw cotton material
khatum	– finished
kurta	– loose shirt worn over churidaars
'La–jwaab'	– exceptional
lungi–style shalwar	– baggy trousers
'Ma jini akal hai'	– 'she's as knowledgeable as an old woman'
Mahabharat	– famous mythological Hindu epic
Mahatma	– sage
mandir	– Hindu temple
methi	– spice known as fenugreek
Mosque	– Muslim place of worship
mullahs	– Islamic priests
'Mummy ne apko chai ke liya bulaiya'	– 'Mummy's invited you round for tea'
nimaz	– Muslim rituals for prayer
Nirvana	– Heaven
nukurdh	– street corner
paan	– betel leaves filled with condiments, used as a mouth freshener
pagli	– mad woman
'Paki'	– racist term used against Asians
pakora	– savoury snack made from gramm flour

pani	– water
puja	– religious ceremony
pukka	– sure, a certainty, authentic
purdah	– veiled
purees	– fried unleavened bread
Ram	– see Ramayan, The
Ramayan, The	– famous mythological Hindu epic about good and evil. Ram Sita, Hunuman and Ravan are the main protagonists in the epic
Ravan	– See Ramayan, The
rotis	– chapattis
shabash	– meaning 'Well done!'
sadhu	– saint
saghan	– a ritual performed to give a good omen for special occasions
'Samji, meri jaan'	– 'Understand, my beloved'
sardar	– a Sikh man
satyagrah	– freedom fight
shalwar kameez	– a long tunic over complementary trousers
Sita	– see Ramayan, The
'Udaas raat hai, zuban pe dard'	– a sad romantic song: 'It's a lonely night, sorrow flows from my lips'
udaasi	– melancholy
Vedas, The	– holy Hindu texts of a scientific nature
vicholi	– go–between
wallahs	– traders
'wog'	– racist term used against Afro-Caribbean and African people
yaar	– familiar friend